ATTACH
MA.

Doctor Sally Preston's relationship with her new chief, Darien Marchmont, got off to a sticky start. So she was less than pleased to discover that their first joint assignment was a two-man medical survey in the heart of the North African desert!

ATTACHED TO DOCTOR MARCHMONT

BY

JULIET SHORE

MILLS & BOON LIMITED
London . Sydney . Toronto

First published in Great Britain 1965
by Mills & Boon Limited, 15–16 Brook's Mews,
London W1A 1DR

© Juliet Shore 1965
This edition 1980
Australian copyright 1980
Philippine copyright 1980

ISBN 0 263 73410 2

Set in 10 on 11½ pt. Plantin

Made and printed in Great Britain by
Richard Clay (The Chaucer Press) Ltd.,
Bungay, Suffolk

CHAPTER ONE

SALLY PRESTON felt like stamping her capably shod foot as she steadily regarded the figure opposite her, playing with a piece of celery on his side plate, as though it was a miniature cricket bat and a discarded piece of cheese the ball.

Sally Preston, or Dr Preston as she was really, fresh from a period of interneship at a famous hospital for tropical diseases in London, was capably dressed from head to foot on this day for a very special reason; she wanted to look capable because she was anticipating an interview with a bigwig belonging to the World Health Organisation, based in London, with a view to securing her next job with that extremely worthwhile body of medicos dedicated to the many and varied needs of member nations, especially the medically backward ones of the world.

She knew she wouldn't land the kind of job she wanted on the strength of ripe-chestnut eyes or sweep of silken-flaxen hair. One had to be on one's toes in the specialised branches of medicine today, especially if one was a woman and, in particular, a pretty woman. Females who would have given their own faces away in exchange for one like Dr Sara Jane Preston's would never believe how she tried to look plainer and often neglected to use make-up so that her mentors might take her opinions seriously rather than smile upon her indulgently and try to date her for her next free evening off duty.

Sally was that anomaly, an extremely attractive

young woman with an earnest desire to know her men friends most intimately on a mental plane. She had been engaged to Tom Rydale, a pathologist, for almost a year. Tom was lunching with her and had just made her extremely angry. Sally always saw everything in black and white and knew exactly what she wanted to do and did it. Tom, she now more than suspected, never quite knew what he did want and so had got around to doing nothing. The idea—or rather Sally's idea—had been that they should apply for jobs to be together under the auspices of W.H.O. For three whole months she hadn't even seen Tom, and it had been almost like meeting a stranger in the restaurant; their kiss of greeting had been self-conscious; Sally had even forgotten what a procrastinator Tom could be.

'Here am I going for my interview and you haven't even applied,' she said rather heatedly. 'I thought it was all decided, Tom. That we——'

'It was you who decided, Sal,' he said mildly. 'You said, "let's do this and that and the other," and I said I would think about it. I'm still thinking about it.'

'Anybody would think you didn't want to be with me. The fact that I may be in Nigeria next week apparently troubles you not one jot.'

Tom proceeded with his table cricket, and Sally knew a moment of terrible truth. Her fiancé really wasn't worried by any thought of further separation. Not only had they forgotten one another's little idiosyncrasies, but Tom had also apparently forgotten that they were supposed to be in love. She tried to tell herself that this wasn't so. Tom hadn't said that. But then, argued her black and white reasoning, Tom would never actually come out with anything so revealing and final. He would haver and dither as he was

6

havering and dithering now about the second most important thing in their lives.

'Tom,' she said calmly, albeit she was anything but calm inside, 'how would you feel if we waived our engagement for a while?'

He gave her his attention immediately.

'Whatever do you mean by that, Sal?' he wanted to know. 'How can one waive an engagement?'

'Well, we could try not being engaged and see what happened. I don't believe in engaged people not seeing one another for months on end, and I'm determined to work abroad for a bit, whereas you obviously aren't keen. It's an awful bore for any man not having his girl available; he feels he can't take anybody else out without having to go into explanations. I shouldn't like you to feel you couldn't take another girl out, Tom, when I'm far away. This past three months has been rotten, somehow, not seeing each other. What do you think?'

'If you loved me ever, Tom,' she silently prayed, 'fight for me now. Say you'll come with me or forbid me to go without you. Say the idea is repulsive to you, that you don't want our engagement to be waived. Say you want to marry me tomorrow or something equally desperate, but please don't temporise with our lives.'

Tom said slowly, 'If that's what you really want, Sal, I won't stand in your way. I wouldn't like to think that you couldn't go out with another bloke, either. It really cuts both ways.'

Sally looked down at her hands, noting that they were clenched, the knuckles white where the skin was stretched tightly. She hadn't been conscious of any tension previously.

'So this is the way Tom and I end,' she thought painfully, 'not with a bang—merely a whimper.'

'If I had a ring,' she managed to say lightly, 'I would return it. But we never did get around to buying that ring, did we?'

'No, we didn't, Sal. I'm sorry.'

'Sorry for not buying me a ring I could return?'

'No, sorry if I've disappointed you, about W.H.O., I mean. I couldn't really see myself matching up to such a job. I'm the sort of chap who likes his rut, Sal. You've always been trying to stir up my ambition, ever since we've been together, and I suppose I've let you down.'

'No, Tom, you haven't let me down. I'm sorry I goaded you. Through your eyes I suppose I'm a domineering sort of female.'

He didn't deny this, and she felt rather nettled. Maybe she *was* domineering and he was relieved to be rid of his obligations.

'We keep in touch, of course?' he asked flatly.

'No,' she said after a moment's thought. 'There's nothing worse than a correspondence between ex-sweethearts.' She spoke as a connoisseur, though her emotions were so new and torn and bleeding she was surprised she could speak at all. 'One must inevitably mind keeping on a friendly plane where one has been involved emotionally, and I know I wouldn't enjoy hearing about your new girl friends one bit. I would be glad for you, but hearing would make me feel a failure. It's best not to drag on . . .'

'I think I would mind hearing about your new men friends, too,' he told her solemnly, and added gallantly, 'who are bound to be legion. But—well, Sal, we can't just say goodbye. Kaput!'

'Of course we can,' she contradicted. 'Let's be the first to end our affair decisively and with dignity. It was nice knowing you, Tom, but it wasn't to be.' She

8

held out her hand, hoping she wouldn't spoil everything by crying at this late juncture.

'Hell, Sal . . .' he said again, havering and dithering to the last.

'Come on!' she urged. 'I have to keep an appointment at two and it'll take me all my time to make it.'

Unwillingly, or so it seemed, Tom gripped her hand and rather spoiled it all by pressing his lips to it. He had never played the courtier with her before and she felt it was a bit late in the day for such displays. Good old plain, stick-in-the-mud Tom she could better understand when he was looking both ways before kissing a girl, rather than seeing him performing continental gallantries in public.

She found herself outside the restaurant and still miraculously in control of her emotions.

'Well, I didn't know *that* was going to happen when I came up to town this morning,' she muttered as she went in search of the parking meter where she had left her lupin-blue little Mini. 'From now on things can only improve.'

But could they?

The London headquarters of W.H.O. were only a mile distant as the crow flew, but the Mini wasn't a crow and had to travel many frustrating road miles before there was the usual crawl in search of a parking space. When she found one being vacated by a peculiar three-wheeled vehicle Sally discovered too late that there really wasn't enough room even for her small car. A red Mercedes ahead was trespassing about a parking meter and a quarter.

Bang! Bump!

'When you've quite finished?' came an angry, masculine voice.

'It's difficult enough parking,' Sally told the brown,

9

sunburned countenance scowling down at her, 'without having *spacecraft* parked alongside the kerb!'

'Is that what you were doing, parking?' the creature asked sarcastically. 'I thought you were trying to climb in.'

'In any case I only banged your bumper,' Sally said heatedly. 'Isn't that what bumpers are for, to bump?'

He smiled in a way which made her temperature rise sharply.

'I will never understand female reasoning,' the stranger said with an air of marvel which insulted the hearer, 'or should that be female *un*-reasoning? Are you capable of handling that lethal weapon sufficiently to allow me to get out, do you think?'

Sally now wanted to cry with mortification, but still she held back and seethed silently, mismanaging the gears so that she thundered forward once more into the red car before finding reverse and wriggling backwards and forwards several times until she—and it—was clear.

'Thanks so much,' the stranger smiled icily. 'I certainly hope you don't bump into me again.'

'That desire is mutual,' Sally blazed back, and added 'good riddance!' under her breath as the Mercedes drew away into the traffic.

She was now late for her appointment. She was to have seen Doctor MacIntosh at two, and now it was twenty past. He took one look at her and forgave her, however. The puir wee lassie looked so put out, and she was certainly a winner. Were they qualifying earlier nowadays, or was it he who was getting auld?

'I think we'll just have a wee cup o' tea while we chat a while,' Doctor MacIntosh decided, donging the bell on his desk and waving the interviewee to a chair. When Sally left the building more than an hour later she had been signed into the service of W.H.O. and was awaiting further instructions. Doctor MacIntosh knew that she was conversant with treatments for various forms of malaria and had also met and dealt with cases of bilharzia, smallpox and typhus. She threw the book of tropical diseases at him and he had smiled as he said, 'Ay, ye'll prove to be a wee smasher, I've no doubt,' thus following the pattern of most of mankind in refusing to take her seriously at face value. She was always having to prove herself, work harder, dig deeper, make a bigger impression because her face was young and fair and her vital statistics pleasing to the masculine eye.

'*He* wasn't exactly impressed with me, though,' she muttered with a certain fierce satisfaction as she remembered the man with the red Mercedes. 'In fact it's the first time any man has hated me on sight.'

The satisfaction died in her bosom as she saw a sticker on the windshield of her car informing her that her stay at the meter was overlong and that she would be required to pay the nominal fine in consequence.

'I shall never bring my car into London again,' she vowed angrily as she drove slowly away into what was developing into early rush-hour traffic. 'I hope my new job takes me far enough away, into the desert, perhaps, where at least there's plenty of room and no parking tickets!'

She little realised at that moment how nearly those hopes were to be fulfilled as time went on.

Sally had decided that sooner or later there must be some violent reaction to the fact that she did not expect to see Tom ever again, thanks mainly to herself who had cleaved the knot so cleanly and with such finality. She had known Tom for the past two years of her training, and drifted into a love affair with him which had seemed pleasant and habit-forming rather than passionate and demanding. But even a pleasant habit cannot be dropped without some sense of loss, and while Tom had been at the other end of a tele-phone line he had had the effect of a sheet-anchor on a trim little craft sailing through shark-infested waters. He had been some safe harbour in which she would eventually moor herself, and now she was adrift on the high seas, sailing without a compass and not knowing where she would eventually ride out the storms of life.

These nautical metaphors exhausted on the Dorking road, Sally decided it would be a relief to discuss the business of the day with Lucy, her friend of many years, who was spending a holiday at Redroofs with the Prestons, father and daughter, and who was also a doctor and between jobs at the moment. Lucy was older than Sally, about thirty to the younger woman's twenty-five, and the salt of the earth.

'She'll find the humour in the situation if there *is* any,' Sally mused, heedless for the first time in her busy young life of the cheery blossoms drenching the country gardens in pink and white snow and the birds trilling for joy of life and living. Now all she wanted was to see the familiar chimneys of home and find both a confidante and a comforter to explain why life had suddenly lost both colour and taste for her.

Surgery had started when she garaged the Mini alongside her father's old Wolseley in the converted stables and entered the house by the side door. Lucy appeared looking somehow feminine, for her, in an at-tractive dress of wild silk. Her brown hair had been trimmed and set. She had a look about her as she had when once she had 'borrowed' Sally's stethoscope out of her duty coat-pocket, having mislaid her own.

12

They both spoke together.

'Sally, I——'

'Lucy, I——'

They hesitated and smiled faintly at each other, then proceeded in concert.

'—wanted to have a chat with you.'

'—have something to tell you.'

'Right,' Sally said quickly. 'Who goes first? Shall we toss up?'

Lucy laughed awkwardly.

'Do you want some tea? Has it been a good trip? Did you get a job?'

'I'm going to get a job and it's been a terrible trip, and yes, I would like some tea. While I'm waiting for it I shall revive myself with a whisky and soda. No, I haven't gone mad, I really need it. Before I start to tell *my* story you'd better get whatever it is off *your* chest. You look like a pickpocket caught in the act.'

'Yes, well——' Lucy guided her friend to a chair, saw that she had an occasional table handy to place her drink on, called to the housekeeper to make a pot of strong tea and then settled herself on the settee opposite.

'Sally, have you noticed anything about me lately?'

The younger woman narrowed her eyes and regarded the other.

'I've noticed you've discarded your trousers, which is a step in the right direction. You really haven't the hips for——'

'Leave my hips out of it. Haven't you noticed anything important?'

As Sally looked blank she said grimly, 'There's none so blind as those who don't want to see. I had hoped I wouldn't have to say it. Sally, I'm in love. It seems to me so terribly obvious that I'm amazed it isn't

13

blazoned all over me.'

'Well!' Sally gasped. This was something she hadn't expected and she felt both pleased and deflated. Lucy had always seemed to her the typical career-woman type. She never had had romantic interludes and had appeared not to miss them. Her career was her all, or so it had seemed until this moment.

'You've certainly bowled me over with your news,' Sally admitted, 'but I think it's absolutely wonderful. Who is he, the lucky man?'

Lucy was a long time answering. She looked down at her big, capable hands and then at the plain court shoes on her feet.

'Your—your father,' she said nervously, at length.

The effect on Sally was startling, to say the least. She looked, first of all, with wide disbelieving eyes as though her friend had taken leave of her senses, then she began to heave and a strange laughter left her lips, a terrifying, mirthless laughter which shook her slight form like an ague and went mercilessly on and on.

The doctor in Lucille Linford acted fast. Her hand struck once, sharply, against the other's soft cheek. Sally's head swung like a ball in flight against the back of the chair, but the laughter ceased and instead a rain of tears poured unchecked down her cheeks.

'Sally, my dear!' Lucy gathered her in capable arms and hugged her close. 'I didn't think you'd take it like this. Nobody wants you to be unhappy. I'll go away and never come back here. Norman—your father— will understand. Please don't cry about it. Don't hate me.'

Sally made watery noises into an inadequate handkerchief and pulled herself away from that smothering embrace.

'Don't play at being my mother too prematurely,'

she said at length, 'and *do* call my father Norman, by all means. If you've got as far as falling in love with him he must have a personal identity, I suppose. You didn't tell me if he loves you. Does he?'

'We—we won't talk about it any more,' Lucy said in her no-nonsense voice.

'Oh, yes, we will,' Sally promptly rebelled. 'You've just given me the shock of my young life. I must have been blind, as you say, but that doesn't mean I want to be a selfish brat into the bargain. My father's comparatively young and attractive and I've always expected to be presented with a stepmother. Forgive me, Lucy, if I didn't expect it would be you. I'll have to get used to the idea by stages. I think it might be rather fun, and I do wish you all the happiness in the world.'

Lucy was looking a little happier now, and kissed her friend tremulously.

'You don't know how relieved I feel, Sally, old thing. I knew it was happening last time I was here and daren't tell you. We—Norman and I—have been corresponding for months. It was awful keeping a secret from you of all people. When you asked me to come down here I could scarcely bear it, wondering how it would feel seeing Norman again. Well, it was wonderful—and this is the result. I wonder if we dare interrupt surgery to tell him you approve? I know he's as worried as I was.'

'I'll slip in on some excuse and let him know the deed is well done,' Sally smiled wistfully. 'I know you'll be good for him, Lucy. You've always been good for me, and we're very alike, Father and I.'

'But why the'—Lucy looked helpless and puzzled—'the hysterics?' she wanted to know. 'That wasn't exactly wholehearted approval, was it?'

Sally smiled faintly.

'On top of everything else that's happened today,' she explained, 'a shock announcement concerning the two people I have left in the world was just what I needed. I simply couldn't absorb it.'

'You have left in the world?' Lucy echoed. 'What's happened between you and Tom? Have you had a row?'

'Just a moment while I slip into the surgery,' Sally said, 'then I can tell you all, as the novels say.'

When she returned Lucy listened in silence, a kind of pleased silence, for she had never liked Tom Rydale.

'—and he just agreed with everything I suggested,' Sally concluded bitterly, 'he didn't raise one little finger to try to hold on to me. Even when I said we wouldn't write he let it go with a shrug and then he—he actually kissed my hand. After all we've been to one another he—he kissed my hand!'

Lucy's tongue peeped from the corner of her mouth and she moistened her lips.

'Can I speak frankly, Sal?'

'Oh, do, by all means,' the other invited tiredly. 'I know you think it's good riddance.'

'So it is. You've discovered today the Tom Rydale that everybody else has known all along. He would walk nineteen miles to avoid one small obstruction in his path. You decided you wanted to work with him somewhere new and exciting, but Tom hasn't your adventurous spirit. He's a stay-at-home-get-his-excite-ment-on-the-telly individual. As long as they'll keep him on at Nick's he'll never change his job. He'll soon know all the patients' blood-counts by heart because they'll always be the same old faces he sees. That's what he likes, sameness and the old routine. He was never for you, Sal. I'm amazed you never saw it before now. And your heart isn't broken; you're just humiliated by having the truth about him forced on you.'

Sally was silent. She was remembering Tom's face across the restaurant table and trying to cry, but tears wouldn't come. Maybe the hurt was only to her pride, and pride didn't bleed.

'You're always pretending to be a dominant personality,' Lucy went on relentlessly, 'but at heart you long to be mastered. You wouldn't respect any man who didn't fight you occasionally, and not only fight but insist on winning.'

Sally sighed, 'I don't think I'll ever want to get married if that's the case. You make marriage sound like a perennial boxing match between uneven combatants.'

'There are compensations in being the weaker sex,' Lucy said placidly. 'We fight in our own way. But tell me about the job. That was your real reason for going up to town today.'

'Funnily enough that has seemed the most trivial item on my day's programme, and yet at one time it was looming so large. I suppose when I'm not so emotional it will be important again. I was formally accepted for service with W.H.O., and I'll probably be sent out to Africa.'

'Africa's a big place.'

'Well, that's all I know, as distinctive from being sent out to India or Arabia. It may be the Congo, or Nigeria . . . who knows?'

'You'll want tropical kit,' Lucy said, trying to rouse the other to enthusiasm, 'so we'll have a wonderful shopping spree together.'

'What are you spreeing about?' Sally asked. Her friend looked hurt and embarrassed and she promptly remembered the big news, and felt remorseful. 'Of

17

course you'll be wanting a wedding outfit and a trousseau. I'm sorry, Lucy, but I still haven't taken all that in. When are you thinking of——?'

Well, we haven't really got down to details yet,' Lucy said happily, 'but Norman wants it to be soon. Dr Robbins is leaving the practice in six weeks' time, so we want to be married and get away together for a bit, then I will be working with Norman. I shall love being a G.P.'

Sally made an excuse to leave the dining-room early that evening so that the sweethearts could uninhibitedly make their plans. Her father, still only forty-seven and young-looking at that, was obviously very happy and could scarcely take his eyes off Lucy's homely face whenever she was in the room. It seemed strange to think of Lucy in this house as its mistress. In a way it would never be the same coming home because it would be Lucy's house; Lucy who would look out her sheets to make up a bed for the guest, for she would feel herself to be a guest rather than the daughter of the house. Of course Lucy would say all this was nonsense and that she would always be welcome, but it would be different and there was no denying it. Lucy might even have children; brothers and sisters for her!

Sally's tired mind boggled at the very idea. She only hoped that soon she would be called away to work. Work was what she needed to take away the stings out of life at the moment, to cushion her losses; for in one day she had virtually lost her sweetheart, her father, her best friend and her home. She was on her own, a wanderer, from now on, on the face of the earth.

CHAPTER TWO

AFTER a week Sally was inclined to agree with Lucy, that her attachment to Tom had been the biggest mistake of her young life. Thanks to those three months of separation she had become inured to not seeing him, but now there was a difference; she was free to see other men, and when her father's assistant, Dr Robbins, suggested taking her up to town to see that zany farce, *Dirty Linen*, she agreed, and enjoyed her evening tremendously. It was improved by the fact that during the interval, when they visited the bar, a surgeon-colleague from her training hospital days introduced her to a he-man type who, he told her, had picked her out as the 'dishiest dish in the stalls'.

'I was flattered to know you,' Alec went on. 'They're girl-starved, you see,' he explained away his companion, 'having just returned from the Falkland Islands, or somewhere equally inaccessible.'

After the show they all went to a party at a nightclub; two other young women had by that time been rustled up from somewhere and in dim blue light, to a very slow waltz, Sally was kissed by the girl-starved meteorologist from the Falklands. She didn't resist; in fact she rather enjoyed it; it was all part of the zaniness of the evening in general, and she was feeling rather man-starved herself. Whatever Tom Rydale had taken from her he had never suspected the well-depths which lay unplumbed within Sally Preston; she didn't really know her own capacity as yet, for either loving or enduring.

That evening served to restore her feminine selfconfidence, however, and she began to bloom again. She had hoped to be away before the wedding, which she fancied might prove embarrassing, the contracting parties being who they were; but this was not to be and she even rang up Dr MacIntosh at W.H.O. to ensure that her appointment was not being overlooked. It was not, he told her, and she would be placed very soon.

The wedding was in church but very quiet, and Sally was surprised to find the service touched her profoundly. She had thought she might mind seeing Lucy standing where her own mother had once stood, beside her father, making the same vows, but instead she felt uplifted beyond resentment. Her father had mourned her mother deeply and long—too long. Now he would never be lonely again in his lifetime, with God's grace, and no true daughter could mind about that.

Neither did Sally mind the post-wedding excitement in the old house with nobody really noticing her, apart from in her advisory capacity. Lucy asked, 'Is this hat too silly for Norway? I do feel a fool in hats,' and Sally told her, 'All respectable married women wear hats in Norway, and if they don't you can always throw it in a fjord.' She knew Lucy was enjoying having her married status emphasised in these first entranced hours and could not resist a little teasing into the bargain. Norman Preston was also in a mild dither. He mislaid the passports and plane-tickets more than once and had to run back into the house for money with a taxi hooting its horn off outside.

'Never make the airport, guv,' the driver was shouting as Sally finally showered the couple with flower-petals and shooed them away with a screeching of wheels.

'Thank heavens one's father isn't doing this sort of thing every week,' she sighed in relief as the house, grown lonely, closed in around her. 'I must get away before they come back, however. I should feel a real gooseberry if Lucy is carried over the threshold to find me still here.'

The letter of appointment arrived the very next morning. She was to be attached to Dr D. E. Marchmont, based at present in Morocco but having a roving commission, his function being to bring health centres throughout North and Central Africa up to date with the most modern treatments and appliances.

Sally had a moment of misgiving. She hoped this Dr Marchmont wasn't an old fuddy-duddy whose doctoring was all done on paper. She wanted true experience, not simply to watch while somebody else did all the work.

Still, Morocco sounded an exciting place in which to start her new job. She had enjoyed holidays in Spain, Yugoslavia and Switzerland and could now ski quite creditably; but on the whole 'abroad' was still a spine-tingling mystery to her. Tropical medicine had fascinated her from the start. There were still so many odious diseases rampant in tropical climes and not yet mastered; many responded to modern treatments, but the problems were social rather than medical. Backward peoples, illiterate and superstitious, still resented incursions into their territories by strangers who wanted to stick needles into them. Somehow they had to be persuaded to want treatment, to refuse to bow with fatalistic resignation to pain, disfigurement and early demise.

Sally not only felt like an eager young doctor rushing to the succour of sick mankind, but also an inspired little disciple spreading the word of Hippocrates' creed.

She spent a pleasant day going through her books and crating those she wished to accompany her wherever she went. Those books contained all the knowledge she would need in her new job. At the hospital she had only come in contact with nice tidy cases of tropical disease which had declared themselves at ports or on ships coming home from far away places, but most diseases she only knew by name, though she felt she would recognise them if she saw them.

While she worked she made up a piece of doggerel which went round and round in her brain all day.

> *I'm attached to Dr Marchmont,*
> *Whoever he may be;*
> *He may be old and fat and grim*
> *And not my cup of tea.*
> *I'm attached to Dr Marchmont,*
> *It says so very clearly;*
> *But how can I be so attached*
> *When I don't know him really?*

The next day she went to town to get herself officially 'kitted up'. She had already been shopping with Lucy and revitalised her private wardrobe with a variety of cool, sleeveless dresses, light mesh shoes and sandals and a couple of cocktail dresses in case there was any social life between W.H.O. officials. Now she bought half a dozen short-sleeved white cotton coats and a new stethoscope. She also called at her late hospital for copies of certificates stating she had been given all the necessary jabs for her travels and then took a taxi to see Doctor MacIntosh for final instructions. Her new appointment was still officially a fortnight hence as her new colleague, Dr Marchmont, was still on leave. She was to report to the hotel El Minzah, in Tangier, at one p.m. local time on June the tenth.

'Everybody knows the Minzah,' said Dr MacIntosh, 'so it's a good focal point. Marchmont will probably tell you what he requires of you over lunch.'

'I really wanted to start immediately,' Sally fretted, and found herself telling the Scotsman about the wedding and her desire to be clear of Redroofs before the honeymooners' return.

'Well, why don't ye take a little holiday, my wee lass?' he asked sympathetically. 'Ye won't get much when ye starrt wi' Marchmont, if I know the blighter. He worrks himself into the ground and all who go wi' him. What's to stop ye staying at the Minzah beforehand? It's expensive but verra cosseting. Oh, aye. Verra, verra cosseting.'

Sally explored the idea as she travelled back into Surrey by train; she had kept her vow not to motor into London since that most uncomfortable experience now nearly three weeks' distant. Of course she could have a holiday in Morocco first; see it as a visitor before she became officially one of the World Health team operating there. The expense of a large hotel was really no deterrent, as her air fare would be paid by W.H.O. and she had been working solidly for eighteen months and was no spendthrift. It was really a very good solution, but if it was to be done then she must act immediately. She put the arrangements for her own personal transportation and that of her car into the hands of a renowned travel agency, who would also see to the hotel booking; then she began to pack, leaving one heavy trunk to follow after her. She began to feel excited and her stomach was a flutter of butterflies when she received confirmation that her flight would be in two stages commencing the evening of May the twenty-eighth, two days distant, when she would take the plane to Gibraltar. The following morning she would cross the Straits of Gibraltar by the Bland Line ferry, the flight situation being rather hazy from the London end at that moment. Her car would follow by the first available air freighter and she was booked into the El Minzah from lunch-time on the twenty-ninth.

How she crammed those last two days with activity! She rang up various friends to tell them what she was doing and also how she and Tom had decided to part. She could tell all this now without emotion of any kind, more as a flat statement, and their murmurs of sympathy she took in her stride. Then she had her hair trimmed to suit warmer climes, but she could not have it shortened, though she did once dally with the idea. Even as a very small girl her long flaxen hair had been the delight of her parents and she had gone to school with two long shining braids. Later she had wound these round her head and now she wore a loose knot, high upon her head, only it was lighter and more manageable because of André's snipping scissors and attention.

Finally she went with Johnny Robbins to the village pub for a final drink. Johnny was holding the fort very ably while his senior was away on honeymoon. Shortly he was leaving the practice to get married himself and join a northern group as a junior partner. The new

Mrs Preston had decided she would rather fill the vacancy than keep house. They had a very good house-keeper already in Mrs Hudd, and Lucy had no inclinations to domesticity.

It was the first time Sally had flown at night and she didn't much like it. For one thing she was too excited to sleep and it felt rather claustrophobic sealed into that dimly lighted cabin with all the immensity of darkness outside. Occasionally there was a light far down; a ship at sea? a lighthouse? Sally couldn't tell. Eventually that 'Attached to Doctor Marchmont' jingle started up in her brain once more and she couldn't stop it. She pictured Dr Marchmont as a desiccated little man with a pinched face and spectacles. If he was noted as a hustler he could not be big and fat and placid. In any case he was merely her boss and she probably wouldn't see anything of him outside of recognised hours of duty. She wondered what the D. E. stood for and tried out combinations of names which might have been popular about the time of the first world war when he was likely to have been born. David and Ernest were possibles as were Douglas and Edwin. She had decided on a combination of Douglas Edward when she drifted into an uneasy sleep and awoke with a start, with instructions from the stewardess to fasten her seat-belt, to find the plane circling the famous rock, jockeying for position to come in to land, in the soft, warm dawn-light of the western Mediterranean.

Fortunately for those concerned, holiday-makers at this exquisite time of year were less prolific than would be the case in six or seven weeks' time. There was room for all on the *Mons Calpe* and, once the bar was open and absorbed its own particular customers, there were even wide-open spaces to be seen both in the saloon and on deck. Sally, who had neglected to either eat or drink a thing for almost fourteen hours, settled for a pot of refreshing tea and a round of buttery toast as she sat looking out over the sparkling sea which at times was grey Atlantic and at others translucent green Mediterranean, as though the waters were loth actually to mix. After early morning sunshine a peculiar grey fog had settled over the township of Gibraltar; a friendly policeman, looking so typically British one looked twice at the brown face and dark eyes under the navy-blue helmet, told her that the mist was a local thing and sometimes stayed for days. He smiled as he said this, for Gibraltarians are a proud people, proud of being British and even proud of their mist; but now the sun had claimed the day and the sea and it was suddenly very hot after England, at least seventy-five degrees Fahrenheit in the saloon, a little cooler on deck because of sea breezes.

After an hour the African coast loomed as Gibraltar receded, but it was another hour before the *Mons Calpe* nosed into her berth in the harbour at Tangier and Sally realised it was the first time she had stepped outside of Europe. There were numerous red-tarbushed gentlemen to prove it, and what must be women, looking like walking grey tents with slits for their eyes, peculiar hostile-looking eyes, who were assembled behind barriers awaiting visiting friends or relations coming off the ferry.

There was a great deal of noise and shouting and a casualness about officialdom, in crumpled uniforms and each person, apparently, armed, which also was not of Europe. Nobody seemed to be worrying or hastening to get the Customs shed cleared or the newcomers on their way. Sally was beginning to fume, standing in a long queue, when a tall, coffee-coloured gentleman examined the labels on her luggage and promptly swept it away.

'Hey! Hey!' Sally called ineptly, trotting behind, and wondering how one said, 'Stop, thief!' in Moroccan, or Arabic, or whatever it was they spoke here.

'Come, please!' the creature bade her rather imperiously, in English. 'I am Mohammed Max. I will take you to El Minzah. Give passport, please. Much quicker for me to do it.'

Sally felt a little disquietude at handing over her passport after her luggage, but Mohammed Max apparently knew what he was about and jumped the queue to present both baggage and documents to gentlemen whom he appeared to know. He waved Sally to join him.

'Quickly, please! We take taxi to hotel.'

Sally was beginning to be glad she had been taken over by Mohammed Max. He was a really splendid figure of a man, at least six foot two, clad in a red tarbush, a long grey cloak, peculiar floppy trousers and curly-toed slippers. The magic words 'El Minzah' were apparently an 'open sesame' to the taxi-driver, too. He, too, was galvanised into life by them and drove at a crazy speed through narrow, winding streets thickly peopled with a cosmopolitan throng composed of visiting British and Americans, Spanish, French and the coffee-coloured denizens accompanied by those disconcerting walking tents she had seen earlier. Sometimes a tent would be pushing a modern-looking pram or pushchair; it was all very strange.

Mohammed Max saw her installed in the foyer of the hotel, paid the taxi-driver on her account with what he said was the usual tip, disdained one of these for himself and disappeared, saying he would see her next day. Sally began to suspect that her new friend worked on a long-term policy and that she would be required to part with plenty of the peculiar-looking money she had acquired on the ferry before she saw the last of him, but she didn't mind, rather liking the fellow and impressed by the fact that he looked clean. His grey robe was spotless and, in his sandals, his feet were well tended and immaculate.

The entrance to El Minzah was unimpressive in an equally unimpressive street, but inside was a different story. There were flights of marble steps and Moorish arches apparently *ad infinitum* leading off in all directions. Sally hadn't really thought much about Moorish architecture before, but found it decidedly Arabian-Nightish and exciting. She was shown to her room on the first floor overlooking that same unimpressive street, but now it looked more impressive from up here because of its busyness and the colourful assortment of its pedestrians; also, opposite her window, there was a fascinating little shop displaying all colours and sizes of curly-toed slippers, beautifully embossed and tooled. She could scarcely wait to buy some for herself and also for Lucy and her father, but it was lunch time and she was hungry. There was only time to wash her hands in her own private bathroom and seek the dining-room, a very handsome room open at one end with a view of a swimming pool and colourful umbrellas under which earlier lunchers were now taking their coffee.

Sally was shown to a small table by a window, for which she was glad, for most of the conversation at the other tables was in French or Spanish, and languages had never been her strong point; also she wanted to absorb the atmosphere and not have to talk. It was while she was investigating a portion of sweet cantaloupe that she saw a beautiful, svelte, dark-haired woman and an equally dark-haired man sweeping down the room in the direction of the pool. Her attention was riveted by the man, for she was convinced she had seen him before, and the fact that she clearly heard the woman say 'darling' made this possible, if they were English. The man turned and raked her momentarily with eyes the colour of steel and she felt the colour rise in her cheeks. Though he looked away the very next moment she felt he too had experienced a prod from memory's finger, and memory was not pleasant. This was the man in the red Mercedes, who had made a bad day so doubly humiliating for her, and whom she had hoped never to see again in her lifetime, let alone here in El Minzah in Tangier. She rather hoped he would glance her way again so that she could cut him dead, but he sailed out into the sunlight, a tall, sunburned and commanding figure of a handsome eagle of a man. Sally decided he would not be allowed to spoil her enjoyment of her lunch and resolutely tucked into the curry she had ordered.

Mohammed Max kept his word by turning up the next day and informing her that he was taking her to see the Casbah and the market. She would much rather have wandered about on her own, for she was finding Tangier a fascinating place, but on the other hand it was difficult to go sightseeing without having a second language proficiently at one's command, and English was little spoken hereabouts. It was Britishers and Americans who apparently kept the guides occupied, and they, on their part, unerringly picked out their next 'victims' and satisfyingly served and fleeced them to the best of their considerable ability.

Mohammed Max had again rustled up a taxi, and in this they went through tortuous ways to the top of the Casbah, and no matter how sinister such places might appear in films, this one looked peculiarly innocent with little brown children and idlers watching all visitors with large-eyed regard. There was a gift shop up here, too, and Sally bought a very nice hold-all for the equivalent of one pound. Mohammed bargained for her and when he considered the price was right he commanded her to pay for it quickly. As a party of Americans were also congregated the local snake-charmer was persuaded to come out of his hidey-hole and put on a performance. An accomplice tootled on a kind of flute and, after much prodding, a tired-looking reptile peeped out of its basket and was persuaded to 'kiss' its keeper. The Americans shrieked in horrified delight at this, but the creature was so tame and so tired that it coiled back into its basket like a damp squib. A collection was taken, but Sally let Mohammed Max understand that she expected more of him than that poor little charade, and so they descended to the Market Place where the horror was real and not contrived. Sweetmeat stalls were black with flies, as was all meat and fish on display. One large fish was alive with blow-flies, their eggs obvious in every fold of the white flesh. Fowls were trussed, waiting with nervous red eyes for the moment of doom; two were decapitated as Sally watched and a rabid-looking dog darted forward and made off with a head in its foaming mouth, and the comb dangling limply in the dust.

'Oh, how horrible!' said Sally. 'All this food about and no hygiene observed. It's terrible.'

A woman edged up to her and plucked her skirt. Unlike most Mohammedan women her face was exposed fully. Her nose was collapsed and she had no upper lip. She whined in a wheedling tone while Sally puzzled over her skin, which had many white patches in the brown.

Mohammed Max burst into Arabic imprecations and almost drove the creature off.

'Give her a dirhem,' Sally instructed, wondering if she was really such a clever and experienced doctor after all when the sight of leprosy had made her quail and, temporarily, feel only revulsion.

'I don't like it here,' she said to the guide, 'and I don't want to buy anything. It has all been very instructive, but I think we'll go back to the hotel now.'

This time she paid Mohammed Max off with a generous fee and tip. He asked her to remember him if she wanted a trip out into the desert or some such treat and she promised she would, but at the moment she was beginning to feel the heat a little and had a strange desire to spend the afternoon in her bed, which, she concluded, would be the beginning of that time-wasting occupation known as taking a siesta, and to which she refused to succumb on principle. Instead she promised herself a swim in that azure-blue pool which, together with the nearby palm-lounge, some of the hotel's guests never left except to eat and sleep. They swam in the pool, lay on canvas beds and dozed off and browned in the sun, rang bells and had tarbushed stewards serve them with snacks and drinks and eventually caught their planes and ships and returned to America, Germany or Switzerland convinced that they had visited Morocco. When Sally thought of that fly-infested market, the remembrance of which still horrified her, she didn't really blame them.

She ate a very light lunch, having decided that one ponderous meal a day was sufficient, and also being a little suspicious of the luscious fruit and sweetmeats, wondering if they had been purchased in that market and been washed and cleaned sufficiently by European standards. Most of the guests had no qualms, however, and also they had apparently acquired the siesta habit and disappeared in ones and twos until only a couple of hardy sunbathers, already browner than the Arabs, occupied the canvas beds strewn about like sanguine flowers on the tough green grass of the lawns surrounding the pool. That had only one occupant when Sally arrived, and he would have to be the man who owned the red Mercedes. Sally would have liked to retreat, but that would have looked too obvious, so she made a great show of removing her wrap and then tried a tentative toe in the shallow end while Leviathan was going up and down, up and down using a fine crawl stroke. As he turned once he gave her a cool nod of acknowledgement, but she had the feeling that this was merely because she was the only other person in the pool and so he could scarcely ignore her. The water was surprisingly cold and she gave a little gasp as she finally ducked, holding her nose. Leviathan now spoke as he turned again at the shallow end, without slowing up.

'I hope your meal is digested?'

As this was formed into a question she felt bound to answer.

'Thank you,' she told him with some satisfaction, 'I do know about such things. I *am* a swimmer.'

32

In case he had been in any doubt regarding her prowess in this sphere she started off in competition, doing her favourite back-stroke. She was surprised to find how rusty she had become, however, and failed to get into the rhythm which had once permitted her to win her heat in the event at an inter-schools championship. She was soon tired and breathless and stopped to rest and regard that monotonously swimming figure going through the water without fuss and with such staying power.

'I suppose he swims back and forth through the Straits and saves his fare,' she pondered acidly. 'Just what *is* he trying to prove? There's nobody to see, only me, and I'm not at all impressed.'

After a rest she began to look towards the diving board. She used to be quite good on a springboard, too, in her swimming heyday, but this was much higher, about ten feet over the water. Still, ten feet wasn't really very high and it wasn't as if she was an absolute beginner.

She climbed the steps and stood on the board, trying it for spring and thinking the water looked a long way off. Diving off from here would be like taking a dive from the deck of the *Mons Calpe*, and she would never have considered doing that. Of course Leviathan *would* have finished his stint for the day at that moment and sit, brown and dripping, on the edge of the bath at the shallow end, apparently content to watch her efforts. Actually she made a very nice picture in her sky-blue bikini. There was nothing too daring about it to offend good taste and her figure was so small and exquisite that there were no unsightly bulges about her. A blue cap covered all but a lock of her blonde hair and she stood well, balanced on her toes and trying to summon up sufficient courage to take the plunge.

She tried to remember the sequence: head between arms, knees rigid, heels touching and relax nothing until one was in the water. She started off all right, but those extra few feet of fall were her undoing. She lifted her head to see where she was going, bent her knees with the idea of going back up again, opened her mouth to shout and hit the water in the most awful belly-flapper of her life. Of course her open mouth took in a lot of water—she was winded anyway, and nature abhors a vacuum—and the muscles felt as though they had been ripped out of her abdomen; she must have blacked out for a moment, because she became aware of a blur which became balconied windows and a canopy of sky as though she had just wakened from an unpleasant dream. She felt sure she was dying and there was a weight like a cement-mixer on her back. Just then she ejected a quantity of pool water and breathed air again. She remembered everything now, the dive and that awful smack as she hit the water. Somebody had lifted her out of the pool and was giving her artificial respiration.

'I—I'm all right,' she managed to groan, and rolled off her stomach, which was killing her. Firm hands felt her over and told her when the bruising had passed she would be o.k.

'Here, you'd better have this.'

Her rescuer thrust a towel at her, and it was then that the full impact of her rashness hit her. The scarlet in her cheeks soon matched the colour of the canvas beds all around, as she looked up swiftly into the grey eyes of the man who had rescued her.

'It's all right,' he said quietly, 'nobody else saw a thing. The Frenchmen'—he indicated the sunbathers—'are asleep and all the curtains are drawn on this side of the hotel. Nobody else knows you were in difficulties, even.'

She looked as though she was going to weep with embarrassment, so he tried to make her angry instead, for she had to react in some way to the shock she had endured.

'You're really not safe out, are you?' he demanded more arrogantly. 'I seem to remember you can't even park a car, let alone drive one, and if you start to dive you've obviously got to finish it instead of turning into a sack of potatoes half way down. You know, the way you're going on, I can't see you making old bones.'

'It's you,' she said fiercely, 'you have that effect on certain people, of whom I must be one. You look so lord-of-all-the-world darned critical that the worst comes uppermost in us. I'm a capable driver and have never bumped any other car but yours in all my years of experience.'

'Which must be countless,' he sneered.

'Yes, well——' she wavered. 'Anyway, you were taking up far too much room on that occasion, and I was nervous.'

She had taken off her cap and her hair fell loosely down and over her shoulders. For a moment his gaze was decidedly appreciative, but she didn't see it, for she was trying to rub herself down without dislodging the towel he had given her.

'I—I think I'll go in now,' she decided.

'Do. You're to have a rest and I'll send the boy with a pick-me-up.'

'No, don't bother. I'm really all right.'

'If you have any qualms about accepting my advice, forget them. I happen to be a doctor.'

35

She looked at him sharply.

'So am I,' she smiled wryly, 'but you must admit that as a breed we make terrible patients and never do entirely what we are told.'

She felt she had rather scored with that, for he looked positively astounded and then smiled ruefully.

'Thanks for the towel,' she told him with dignity, 'and thank you for—for everything. Somehow one can't say more than that.'

'I was glad to be of service.'

She walked away feeling limp but trying to maintain her poise. After collecting her wrap and rubber slip-slops she went up to her room and lay trembling on the bed. A steward tapped and entered carrying a large glass of brandy.

'I am to give Mademoiselle zis,' he announced, 'with compliments of Monsieur le Docteur.'

'Thank you,' Sally said gratefully, and swallowed her pride along with the energising, fiery draught.

CHAPTER THREE

SALLY was rather relieved than otherwise when 'Monsieur le Docteur' left El Minzah next day. She was passing through the foyer on her way to the post-office when she saw a heap of luggage and an apparently irritable but gloriously lovely young woman tapping her well-shod toe with some impatience beside it. A moment later the Mercedes man joined her and she said sharply, 'Darien, you're *always* keeping me waiting. The plane will *not* wait, as you well know.'

Darien (what a name! thought Sally) murmured something placating and they moved out to the red Mercedes, which a steward had been polishing to shining perfection in the meantime. Sally hung back until it had moved off, for she still felt embarrassed whenever she remembered that incident in the pool. She hadn't used the pool since, but determined to do so, so as not to develop any psychological dread of water, though she would be content to take a header in from the side in future.

She thought of the couple who had just left, thinking what a handsome picture they made together. She presumed they were married, as the woman was possessive to that degree married people usually are. The car lent to her imagination a certain opulence of means, as did the cream pigskin luggage, all matching down to the small vanity case the woman carried herself; also it must cost twice as much for two people to stay at the Minzah, and it was certainly expensive enough for one. Sally had discovered that it was fatal to order anything which had to be imported. An innocent bottle of Coca-Cola, one afternoon, had cost her the equivalent of fifty pence. She kept to the local wine and water after that, and of course, cups of coffee which were excellent. The tea-bag tea she did not relish but the food was rich and well-cooked, though monotonous after the first few days.

Just occasionally Sally felt the stirrings of loneliness. If Tom had been there it would have been extremely pleasant; or even if Lucy had been available instead of having suffered a sea-change and become her stepmother, somehow putting herself outside the pale of their former friendship and companionship. A pleasant young Gallic gentleman had tried to befriend Sally in the Palm Court one day, but the language barrier had defeated them both, and Dr Preston did not exactly like being 'picked up', even in a broadminded place like Tangier. She was now looking forward to getting down to work. Lotus-eating was all right in small doses, but could soon blanket one in satiety if one had no serious occupation.

She was distracted out of her boredom by receiving notification that her car was now in Tangier and would need clearing by the Customs authorities. She had already been advised by an ancient Briton, a very charming literary gentleman who was more or less a permanency in Tangier and came to the El Minzah for occasional meals, that she would do well to apply for a Moroccan driving-licence. This she had now done. There had been no test of competence required, and this didn't amaze her after seeing the way the city's taxis careered around the streets. She went off happily with Mohammed Max to collect her car; he was going to steer her through the intricacies of getting it into

38

her possession for the pleasure of riding back home in it. Gentlemen of Max's calibre did not own their own cars, but there was nothing they enjoyed better than to cadge a ride and then shriek at all their friends through the open windows.

Mohammed Max was certainly a good friend to possess in Tangier; he seemed to have an easy acquaintance with all authority and know exactly what must be done to oil the wheels of sluggish officialdom. He took charge of Sally's cigarette case and lighter and handed them round the Customs shed freely, not forgetting himself, taking great pleasure in clicking at the little model lighthouse and exclaiming each time the flame was successfully ignited. All the while the rich grunts and throat-clearings of his native Arabic poured out, creating mirth among his audience. He broke into English to command Sally to replenish her cigarettes as soon as possible as they were all gone, but these high-handed tactics appeared to have paid off, for out of scores of newly impounded motor-vehicles, of every make and size in the motoring world, Sally watched her little blue Mini make its bow to the Arab world, its headlamp eyes round and startled and cosily familiar.

Now she had a friend who could go exploring with her. Once more life would be fun.

But before her friend could be of service to her it had to be manhandled as far as the nearest petrol pump. Somehow between London and Tangier half a tankful of petrol had been siphoned away. Mohammed Max clucked up a couple of little boys who did all the work for one dirhem, however, while Sally steered and the lordly one shouted instructions and imprecations which would have been recognisable in any language.

Moroccan petrol was a bit smelly but quite serviceable and Sally felt happy even though she was driving on the unfamiliar side of the road. Mohammed Max directed her miles out of her way, and she knew it, before he finally announced that he lived a little way off down the next turning. Sally didn't mind the jaunt as it had served to break her in to the hazards of driving on a new—or rather very old—continent. Mohammed Max now trotted off to have his siesta, after directing her back to the hotel. They were now in the dock area and she found all she saw fascinating. A couple of trim yachts were tied up at their moorings and there was both Moorish and modern American folk-music pouring from sidewalk cafés. She parked the car and drank great gulps of sea air, half perched on a little wall in the shade of a small cargo ship taking on fresh fruit and vegetables for rocky little Gibraltar.

Suddenly Sally thought she was seeing things as she saw a girl's head lying in a patch of sunlight on the dusty road ahead. At first the head appeared to be disembodied because it was a blonde head, as fair as her own, though perhaps not quite as natural. She stirred herself to action as she saw a little group of young men huddle round the girl and attempt to pull her to her feet.

'I'm a doctor,' Sally announced herself. 'Can I help? Is anything wrong?'

'No, nothing's wrong, Doc,' said one of the young men in an American accent, though Sally knew that American accents do not necessarily belong to Americans. This fellow looked either Italian or Maltese; he hadn't the hauteur of the true Spaniard and he was also inclined to flabbiness. Perhaps he was even Greek.

'As a matter of fact, Doc,' said a more Anglicized voice, though its owner looked pure Arab, 'the poor

40

darling's been going at the bottle a bit heavily for the time of day. We're just taking her home. She'll sleep it off.'

The girl groaned and emanated alcohol. Sally winced, for she didn't look a day over nineteen. For a horrible moment the thought dawned on her that this cosmopolitan group could be engaging in white-slave trafficking right under her nose, but the girl opened her eyes and made a grab at the whitest-skinned member of the group, who had pale platinum hair and wore large square sun-glasses.

'Oh, God, Jerry, I'm going to be sick. Get me to bed.'

Bed was apparently aboard one of the yachts, for the group moved off down an adjacent slipway, half carrying the girl among them. One of the young men turned back to nod in Sally's direction and said something apparently uncomplimentary like 'Interfering dames!'

'If that's the way the idle rich behave I'm not sorry I've got to work for my living,' she decided in disgust. 'That girl's liver when she's forty—if she lives that long!'

When she returned to her car she found a most sinister thing had happened. Two of her tyres were savagely slashed almost into ribbons.

She enquired of nearby loungers, but they turned away, not understanding. She was getting nowhere fast, unable to cope with such an unpleasant situation on her own, when she thought to mention the magic words 'Mohammed Max', and showed a small, sore-eyed boy a five-dirhem piece. The boy darted off and eventually, just as Sally was beginning to despair, came back with a harassed-looking Mohammed Max in tow. He had been hauled from his bed, not wearing his fine grey cloak but a ragged shirt, in which he still managed to look dignified, and took the five dirhems from her hand, scolding, 'Too much for such small service,' handed the boy what he thought fitting, pocketed the five dirhems for himself and surveyed the damage speculatively.

Sally pointed at the watching crowd.

'Find out who's responsible,' she said angrily. 'I was attending to a sick person and they did it behind my back. One of them,' she insisted accusingly.

Mohammed Max became extremely haughty and offended.

'Not my people,' he said sharply, 'do such things. They do not destroy. They are quite happy to steal from you. If you do not lock car, they will take rug, purse, but damage? No.'

'Then—then who would?' Sally asked faintly.

Mohammed Max looked round for someone who was not apparently to be seen.

'White people do such things,' he told her. 'I see American film.'

'But films aren't real,' she said sharply. 'This is.'

Still, she felt happier to have an aide at such a time. Her companion set his own private rescue team to work. An ancient lorry arrived and the spare wheel was put in place of the damaged rear one and the car jacked up to the lorry. Somehow the whole works was transported to a garage and Sally herself put into a taxi.

'For my services, Madame,' said Mohammed Max, and named his price. Sally paid without argument, feeling very depressed about the whole business. Why had somebody done that to her? It was so unnecessary; so *unkind*.

'Madame,' Mohammed Max said playfully, 'I think now you should know that whatever I ask you must pay me only half.' He said 'half' as 'haff'. 'Only half. You understand? That is the way.' He pressed a cluster of dirhems into her hand and told her how many to give the taxi-driver. That was the best moment she had known in quite a few bad hours and she appreciated it as an oasis in the desert.

Once her car was returned to her with two new tyres, Sally quickly forgot the unpleasant incident and convinced herself that such a thing wouldn't happen to her again. She enjoyed a run south over the desert road to Marrakesh, Mohammed Max accompanying her to see that damage came neither to the car nor herself in that order. When they passed a camel encampment the guide was all for her having a ride out into the desert by such means. Business was apparently poor on this particular day, and the camel owners thought it a bit thick that Mohammed Max, their friend from the city, should not be able to produce one customer at least for them.

Sally, however, thought the camels looked rather terrifying and they were much bigger than she had imagined them to be; also they looked somewhat moth-eaten under their colourful saddle-cloths. Their haughty expressions and long-lashed eyes gave the lie to their extremely bad-tempered grunts, and so she kept her distance and urged Mohammed Max to finish his conversation and allow them to get on.

The guide, however, had touched upon the fact that his 'client' was a doctor. He was extremely proud of this fact since he had discovered it, for in his eyes it made up for her being a woman. A Moslem woman is not the most highly regarded of Allah's creatures and foreign women are usually only tolerated because they are able to pay a man for his services. This eccentricity cannot be overlooked when a man has his living to earn, and Mohammed Max found he went down rather better with white women than their menfolk. Of the little lady doctor, however, he had become quite fond. She paid his dues without argument, these now being half of what he asked. Once she had even given him a third of his asking price, reminding him that he had done the same service for her only two days ago and the cost of living simply couldn't have gone up since then. Such astuteness pleased him and he felt she would soon be able to get along without him.

Now, however, he suggested she might take a look at one of the cameleer's feet which was giving him a little trouble. Sally despaired of making Mohammed Max understand that she could not go around treating people without the necessary authority. She was '*hakim*' and he did not want to know about ethics or such tarradiddles. Out here, miles from anywhere, was a creature in pain. She was the doctor, so she must go ahead and prove herself. As she still hesitated he asked her if she would stand idle if they came upon a motor accident with bodies lying all around in states of terrible injury.

'Of course not,' she said indignantly, 'but there are clinics, and your friend should have attended one of those. This is *not* an emergency.'

Mohammed Max told her most severely that it was a most dire emergency for Suleiman to take time off from his job. Who would feed and water his camel or attend to his customers for him?

Sally remarked that she couldn't see any customers from where she was, but it was a losing battle and she knew it. Saying it was the very last time she would be talked into doing such a thing she looked at Suleiman's foot. It was grubby and a large splinter was embedded in a cradle of pus. A local anaesthetic did little to deaden the pain of her probing, and she knew this, but Suleiman was a stoic and not one whimper escaped his lips as she finally withdrew the offending splinter, together with an explosion of blood and pus, wrapped a dressing over the whole, which she stuck down with Elastoplast, gave him a large injection of slow-acting penicillin and instructed him to attend a clinic to have the dressing changed within two days.

Suleiman was most grateful and wanted her to have a free ride on his camel in payment. She now knew better than to refuse an Arab gift out of hand, but thanked him mightily and asked if he would remember his offer when she was next that way. She did not want to drive over the desert at night and already they were much delayed, as he would understand.

This trip was really the end of her holiday, for tomorrow was June the tenth and she had pencilled in her diary that she was to lunch with Dr Marchmont in the hotel at one o'clock. She had already told the Ancient Briton, who had taken to joining her whenever he ate at El Minzah, that she most regretfully had requested to be placed at her senior's table on this occasion.

'And then I don't know where I'll be. Not at El Minzah, I feel sure.'

'No, I shouldn't think World Health runs to that. Marchmont is a regular visitor, but then he has private means, I believe.'

'Oh,' Sally responded. She was curious about her new boss, but battened down the desire to find things out about him by back-door methods. She would soon know all she needed to know about him.

On the morning of the tenth she finally succeeded in getting a handsome leather pouffe case dispatched to

England as a present for the honeymooners, together with some slippers. She had received letters from both of them. Her father was 'very happy and grateful for a second chance of such happiness'. Lucy said even less and managed to convey more. 'I never knew what I was missing. Can't you make things up with Tom?'

Dear old Lucy! She was so happy she wanted everybody else in her circle of acquaintance to rake out their old love affairs and share her enthusiasm for marriage. But Tom was a poor dead fish. He had made no effort to reach her, as far as she knew, but had quietly accepted her ruling that a clean severance was to be preferred to a protracted withdrawal.

She drove back to El Minzah in good time for lunch. It was very hot, today, at least eighty-five degrees Fahrenheit in the sun, and she had a headache. It was a pity that she did not feel her best when she was due to meet her senior colleague for the first time. Outside the hotel entrance was the red Mercedes with the same small boys polishing it.

'Oh, no!' groaned Sally, not caring to see that particular gentleman again. Of course it could be another Mercedes, but the number plate did look familiar, though she had never actually memorised it.

In her agitation she had omitted to make the handbrake of her own car absolutely functional. The vehicle slid forward on the slightly sloping street and there was a crash of bumpers.

'Oh, no!' cried Sally even more agitatedly as one small boy darted into the hotel to announce the news with gamin joy while the other ran around like a disturbed ant.

Sally backed her car away, this time pulling the handbrake well forward. As she climbed out she was aware of that ominous presence on the hotel steps, the grey eyes, the aloof, disapproving expression as though she was something which had rather gone off its freshness.

'Good morning!' he greeted acidly. 'I see we've met again with our usual exuberance?'

'Well,' Sally said defensively, 'I don't think there's any damage. Is there?'

'Not if you're still of the opinion that bumpers are meant to bump. I like mine twisted and dented. Actually I think it's rather fetching.'

She bit her lip to restrain the angry retort which trembled there. She was in the wrong yet again and must expect to have her nose rubbed in the dirt. He was that sort of man.

'There is a very small dent,' she informed him, 'and I hope you'll let me pay for having it hammered out.'

He was squatting looking under the car.

'That sort of thing does one's big end no good.'

'Well, any damage——' she hesitated, wondering if her means would stretch to having a big end repaired. She wasn't very sure what it was.

'So may I go now?' she asked politely. 'I have an appointment. Would you like my name and address?'

'No, *thank you*,' he said with some emphasis. 'If you tell me where you'll be next week I shall do my best to travel in the opposite direction. I shall let you off for that information.'

She didn't know whether he was laughing at her or not, but decided to reply seriously.

'I'm afraid I don't know where I'll be next week. My plans are in a state of flux.'

'That follows,' he said almost kindly. 'Run along and keep your appointment. I shall—watch out for you in future.'

Her cheeks were scarlet with mortification as she

47

went up to her room, but mercifully her headache had gone.

'Who would have thought *he* would turn up here again?' she asked as she did her hair afresh and regarded herself in the dressing-table mirror. 'I wouldn't mind if he didn't make me appear such a nitwit. I suppose he tells his wife about our encounters and makes her roar with laughter. I suppose she nearly had hysterics when he told her about the diving episode.'

It was now five past one and she had no more time for embarrassing reminiscence. She ran downstairs and paused in the smoking-room, a magnificent apartment furnished with luxurious Persian rugs, bright leather pouffes and brass prayer tables now used for holding coffee cups and ash-trays. There were only two people in the room, for guests were now sitting in the dining-room, service being inclined to be slow at the Minzah.

'Where have you got me, Ali?' Sally heard the voice she had learned to dread ask, and fell back into obscurity behind a Moorish screen.

'Table number three, Dr Marchmont,' Sally heard the head waiter reply, then there was an exchange in Arabic, laughter, and both voices faded down the long room.

Sally stood as though rooted to the spot. Oh, no! *That* man couldn't be the Dr Marchmont to whom she was to be attached! It would be too cruel of fate to do this thing to her. Yet hadn't they met, or rather crashed, originally, in the vicinity of the World Health Organisation in London? Also he had told her he was a doctor, had treated her as any doctor would when she had nearly drowned herself. His companion had called him Darien, so that accounted for the D in the D. E.

Marchmont. Why hadn't she suspected the truth previously, played a little more safely with this man? It would be virtually impossible to work with the man now, after all that had happened. He would probably refuse to have her on his staff.

'He can't sack me for bumping his wretched car,' Sally comforted herself, 'or for needing rescuing. He doesn't know what I can do as a doctor.'

She braced herself and stepped forth into the dining-room, pretending she didn't know where she was to go and putting herself in Ali's charge. The head waiter asked her to follow him and announced her ringingly, so that Sally felt the whole dining-room must be aware of her discomfiture. The tall figure of Darien Marchmont suddenly loomed up, blotting out the light from a whole window. Something like a sigh escaped him and she decided he was well-mannered above his personal feelings.

'*Do* sit down, Dr Preston,' he said sweetly, 'and let us count our blessings in this reunion. They must be around somewhere. For one thing we have actually met without incident for once. Perhaps this is a happy augury and we should neither of us be too dismayed. At any rate you always look most attractive about your unfortunate business, which is some consolation, I suppose. What shall we drink? And if you say "hemlock for one" I shall be most disappointed in you.'

CHAPTER FOUR

SALLY found herself lost for words. She suddenly felt the need to remember that this man was, from this day forward, her boss, her medical mentor. He could say, 'Do this, Dr Preston', or 'Go there, Dr Preston', and it behoved her to say 'Yes, sir', or 'Immediately sir', without argument. This man had it in his power to make or mar her career in the immediate future. Having innocently wrong-footed herself with him on so many occasions, she must now swallow her pride and allow him his moods, like tides, until there was smooth water between them once more.

'Look here, sir,' she now tried, 'I know you must mind about it being me here in this capacity. I don't know why we didn't guess earlier.'

'I know why *I* didn't guess,' he returned sharply, 'because I went to London especially to request the powers-that-be to hand-pick my assistant on this occasion. I told them exactly what I wanted and specified it should be a likely young lad. Now nobody could call you *that*, Dr Preston.'

She blushed and almost forgot her new resolution.

'You can blame me for two minor collisions and one foolish exhibition,' she said warmly, 'but not for my sex—er—sir. I have so far been found competent in my work, at least. Maybe there wasn't a "likely lad" in stock and so they gave you a "likely lass" as being next best, though my blood boils to say it.'

'Spoken like an ardent little feminist,' he now applauded. 'A sex war in the middle of the Sahara is just what I need, I don't think. I like women, Dr Preston. I love 'em. I like their perfumes, their feminine foibles, their wiles, their pretty shimmery clothes; even their lunatic reasoning of which you gave me a shining example. Bumpers are meant to bump, indeed! But the ideal situation of one of these delicate blooms, no matter how bursting with erudition she may be, is not beside me in the middle of nowhere getting bitten by sandflies, or shuddering with malaria, or sharing the same blanket at night when the truck has broken down five hundred miles away from anywhere. What would your dear mother say to that?'

'I haven't a mother,' said Sally flatly, 'and my new stepmother, who is only five years my senior, would laugh herself sick over any of these predicaments.'

He looked at her almost admiringly with those direct, steel eyes of his.

'I think you have a most unfeminine sense of humour, perhaps, Dr Preston?'

'Women have been known to be amused on occasion, sir.'

'If you had been the "likely lad" I was expecting you'd have been kicked where it hurts before now. Perhaps you had better put those quick wits of yours to sorting out this mess, Dr Preston. My entourage is not equipped to accommodate a young and attractive woman. You're a very real problem.'

'Perhaps if you began to think of me as a doctor, sir, the problem would be halved for a start? The young and attractive woman is well tucked away inside a serious medical practitioner. I have absolutely no interest in the opposite sex at present.'

'You amaze me,' he said faintly. 'It's to be hoped

that the opposite sex develops no alarming interest in *you*. However, I can see you're a determined young lady, and that I must seriously consider you in the role of my assistant. In fact there is no time to replace you. Tomorrow we move off at dawn. What clothes have you?'

'Er—clothes, sir? The usual for warm climates. Light dresses and sandals; that sort of thing.'

He began to scribble on a page torn from a note-book, writing from right to left of the page, which made Sally stare.

'It's all right,' he smiled. 'Actually my Arabic is rather more legible than my English. Your afternoon is now decided. My servant will take you to this ad-dress where you will equip yourself with breeches, shirts, hose and boots and also something to cover your head. Don't be surprised if the garments with which you are supplied bear the mark of either Her Majesty's or French Government forces. Ask no ques-tions. Yussef will pay. I'll take the liberty of putting your car alongside my own in dry dock for the time being.' He saw her countenance drop and explained, 'Where we're going we'll fare much better in a truck. Unfortunately we can't always take roads with us. You didn't think you were going to be billeted in a nice little hospital with electric fans and the telly, did you?'

'I didn't know what I was going to do, sir. This is my first post with World Health. What exactly does this safari of ours entail?'

He smiled.

'A good name for it. Well, as you know, member countries in the Organisation are entitled to medical know-how and help. They prefer their own nationals in actual contact with patients, and so there is a scheme afoot to train doctors and nurses to man clinics and hospitals. Although there is a lot of leeway to make up in the matter of fully trained personnel, there are now fewer and fewer Europeans working outside of Europe, in the Organisation, apart from administrative centres such as at Brazzaville, in the Congo. But they do love to send Europeans out on sorties such as ours gathering the gen and pumping it out to fill the pages of the monthly "Epidemiological and Vital Statistics Report". We are bent on a fact-finding mission to discover, among other things, if there is still much typhus incidence in North Africa; if, in fact, there is now resistance to insecticides such as D.D.T. You know that the rabbit population which survived myxamatosis is now thriving? Well, if lice are equally now immune to known insecticides we may again expect epidemics of typhus. Our information is passed to the lab boys and they get busy devising another and, it's to be hoped, more permanent deterrent. To make our trip rather more hilarious, we're not required to examine urban areas, however. The wide blue yonder is always our destination; the village without a drainage system, the Bedouin encampment, a corpse in the desert leaving a trail back to an infected water-hole. That's the general idea. Any comment?'

Sally was feeling rather disappointed.

'It sounds like all paper-work and no doctoring,' she opined.

'My dear girl, you're joking: I went on a similar mission earlier in the year, fact-finding about malaria, which is the Organisation's most expensive complaint and is still far from being eradicated. I toured Ethiopia and Saudi Arabia on that occasion. My fact-finding was comparatively easy, but it was only to be rumoured that a doctor was in the vicinity for all the halt, maimed, pregnant and merely interested to descend on my encampment from miles around. Those who weren't in need of attention had relatives who were, who couldn't travel, who lived "just a step up the road" and were more likely to reside twenty or fifty miles away over rough country and who had probably been around in Adam's time in any case. You'll do more doctoring than you can probably cope with, my likely lass, so cut and run while the going's good, if you think you can't take it.'

'Pooh!' was Sally's prompt response to this. 'I'm not very big, but I think I'm tough. I'll just have to find out.'

'Good!' He was now ever so slightly approving of her, she fancied, and she knew she had to work hard to overcome a rather sorry beginning. She knew she wasn't the fool he was inclined to think her, but this would have to be proven.

The rest of the meal passed in more general conversation; they spoke of plays they had seen in London which they had either loved or loathed.

'And how is Mrs Marchmont?' Sally asked politely in conclusion.

He glanced at her sharply. 'Thriving, thank you. She gives me no cause for anxiety, bless her!'

'So he's happily married,' Sally decided. She thought it best not to ask after any possible little Marchmonts. This first encounter was not the occasion for a heart-to-heart, and he might consider her inquisitiveness founted from a desire on her part to soften him up.

'Perhaps I'd better go and do my shopping now, sir?' she asked when they had finished coffee.

'Yes. Be in the foyer in ten minutes and I'll introduce you to Yussef.'

He stood while she rose, collected her handbag and

moved off. She felt his eyes watching her progress down the long room. Perhaps he was thinking what a little thing she was, for he was so tall; about six foot three with a deep chest, though surprisingly narrow hips. She had always regretted not being taller. Lucy, who was a comfortably built five foot eight, comforted her by saying that good stuff went into little room. Her father had once called her his 'fairy', and perhaps she had always wanted to prove that lack of inches would be no deterrent to making her way in the world.

She was in the hotel foyer in only seven minutes and picked up a British newspaper which somebody had left on the desk. She hadn't bothered with newspapers herself during her holiday; someone in the next room to her own had a transistor radio and listened faithfully to the B.B.C. each evening, a programme which Sally rather unwillingly overheard, so she knew there was no national news of terrible import to worry over.

Now she found her eyes riveted to the page in front of her. There was a picture of a young, blonde woman and an even blonder man, screwing up his eyes. Both were tanned and wearing beach clothes. It could be any couple from any holiday beach in the world, but the letters glaring in Gothic script from the adjacent column were by no means ordinary:

HAVE YOU SEEN THIS GIRL? they demanded.

Sally read on:

'Melinda Lycett-Houth, daughter of property-magnate Wynford Lycett-Houth, aged nineteen, has disappeared from St Aubrey's Finishing School for Young Ladies near Berne, Switzerland. Melinda, who was prevented from going through a form of marriage with Jeremy Ripon, also pictured, at Gretna Green last year, who is since known to be a married man, may have been abducted by him, as the girl's father has now received a note demanding a considerable sum of money for her safe return. This is being treated by the police as a case of kidnapping, and there is a reward of £1,000 for any information regarding the whereabouts of Miss Lycett-Houth or Mr Ripon.'

Sally looked again at the picture and her stomach felt queasy and most uneasy.

'Well, Dr Preston, this is Yussef. He will——'

'Oh, Dr Marchmont, I've seen this girl and this man here in Tangier. What must I do?'

Darien Marchmont looked idly at the picture.

'Calm down for a start,' he advised her. 'You're going to have a busy afternoon. Do there *have* to be complications? You're a young woman with a fairly lively imagination. Now ask yourself if you're sure about this. It's a rotten sort of picture.'

Sally looked at the picture a little more doubtfully.

'The girl I saw was blonde, but she was so drunk and looked so ill I couldn't really be sure, I suppose. But the man was the same, only he was wearing dark glasses.'

'Dr Preston!' The voice was getting decidedly impatient now.

'I'm sorry, sir. I could be wrong. I—I'm ready to go.'

'And about time. We have no time to get involved with either politics or police. Please try to stay clear of trouble for my sake if not your own.'

He didn't believe a word of her story, Sally concluded as she climbed into a smart little jeep beside Yussef, Dr Marchmont's personal servant and co-driver. His disbelief made her not believe herself. What a fool she would have looked running to the police with her story only to find she had implicated absolutely innocent people and started a false trail!

56

They would think she was after the reward, which didn't interest her in the least and which she would have donated to a worthwhile charity in any case.

Yussef did not speak English so they had a quiet drive down to the dock area, near where her own car tyres had been slashed. In a back alley Yussef introduced her to a swarthy gentleman who looked like a human eagle, his nose was so fiercely hooked between hard, black little eyes. He was not dressed in the loose robe or floppy trousers of the Moroccan national, and Sally concluded he was either of India or Pakistan, those inveterate traders who turn up in every corner of the world and to whom no country's currency is ever a mystery.

Mr Bulchand *did* speak English and took Sally into a small room where there were clothes and uniforms of all descriptions. She could find no breeches to fit her, but she did find four pairs of jodphurs in her size, two in cotton and two in cavalry twill. The bush shirts were also on the big side, but they could be belted in, and she took rather a fancy to them with their accommodating masculine pockets and shoulder straps. One pair of chukka boots and one pair of brogues; four pairs of knee hose and an Australian bush-hat. She felt like the League of Nations as she finally left Bulchand's and looked around while Yussef paid the bill with much altercation and argument.

She bought a coloured postcard and a stamp from a nearby pavement vendor, and wrote the information home that she would be pushing off on the morrow, leaving an accommodation address for mail. As she looked around for a place to post it, she saw a lounging figure which struck her as familiar. She went up to the young man, who now looked wholly Arab to match his coffee-coloured countenance, and asked: 'Was your friend all right? You know, the girl who was ill?'

The sepia eyes regarded her warily.

'You told me she had had too much to drink,' Sally proceeded patiently. 'It was almost a week ago. You took her down to a boat over there.'

The eyes were veiled now, hostile.

Yussef called, 'Hakim?' and seeing her, trotted over.

'Just one moment, Yussef,' Sally turned to say, knowing he would understand her mime if not her words. When she looked around the young fellow she had been questioning was travelling at a steady lope down the street.

Now Sally *knew* there was something fishy going on. Nobody was going to talk her out of following up her suspicions.

'Yussef, come!' she commanded, pointing to the jeep, and set off in pursuit on foot. Her quarry left the open street and darted into an alley way, then another, until Sally was going she knew not whither, and only saw that each street was meaner and more sinister-looking than the last. She had lost him. She paused to look round in the half light, her heart thumping, and then a blow on the back of the head caused her to hit the cobblestones in a blaze of fireworks. She heard footsteps running away and then Yussef crying, 'Hakim! Hakim!' and tugging at her to get up.

Her senses came back fully though her head was splitting.

'Please take me back to Dr Marchmont.'

Somehow she staggered back to the jeep, shaken and shocked, and continued to sit there while Yussef sought out his master and told him his version of the afternoon's goings on.

Sally did not know how pale she was looking, how only the thickness of her braided hair had prevented her skull from being fractured. Darien Marchmont took one look at her, scooped her up as though she was a bag of shopping, carried her up to his room and dumped her on his bed, sending Yussef to order a stiff brandy.

'Tell me, as soon as you can, what happened,' he said as he cleaned her scalp and put a dressing over the wound. She drank the brandy obediently and then had a little weep. This over, she told him exactly what had occurred.

'Perhaps you'd better tell me about the other business—the drunken girl, etc. There may, after all, be some connection with the hoo-ha in the papers.'

Again Sally told him all she knew, described the men and the girl, remembering what they wore, and how the girl had asked 'Jerry' to get her to bed.

'After that I was distracted by finding two of my tyres slashed,' she said in conclusion. 'Getting help and having my car towed to a garage took me all afternoon. I was utterly fed up. It was a wicked thing to do.'

'Perhaps you had stumbled upon wicked people who tried to foil your interest in them. I think we must tell the police, after all.' He sighed hard.

'Are you angry?' she asked in a small voice.

'Furious,' he told her, making her heart plummet earthwards once more. 'Nobody coshes a member of my staff without arousing my basest instincts. I'll have somebody's blood for this if it's the last thing I do.'

For that Sally felt a little better. She was now a member of his staff and he was prepared to take up cudgels on her behalf. That was really very nice of him. When he left her for a little while he returned to find her asleep like a kitten on his bed, one hand clasped under her cheek and the other dangling limply floorwards.

'Watch the door,' he instructed Yussef. 'Let her sleep it off. We'll never get off tomorrow now, so we might as well settle our minds on that score.' To himself he continued, 'How does she do it? Is it a gift, or what? She manages to look like a schoolgirl, all rose-petals and dewy-eyed, and then she raises the very devil. I've never known a moment's peace since she crashed into my life. She's an appealing little thing, though, and I can see this next trip having its livelier moments. If we ever get started, that is.'

CHAPTER FIVE

ANOTHER week passed before they were free to start their undertaking, a week of frustrating idleness for Darien Marchmont and equally frustrating busyness for Sally. She attended the Police Department at least a dozen times, telling the same story over and over again without anybody, apparently, doing anything about anything apart from drinking interminable cups of strong Turkish coffee and smoking very strong cigarettes.

'If only I could speak direct to London myself!' Sally sighed in despair after one such interview. 'Do you think I could? Why not?'

'For one thing,' Darien Marchmont said sharply, 'you would be stepping so hard on police toes that they would probably keep you here for months in retaliation, and for another you can't just call up London, like that, in a place such as Tangier. You would be required to book your call, hang around, and anything from thirty-six hours to five days later you might, possibly, be called to the instrument to hear a distant gnome, with hiccoughs, trying to make sense out of you. The game just isn't worth the candle.'

Sally felt that her senior colleague was more than a little fed-up with her. Not only had he asked for a 'likely lad', and been landed with her, but he seemed to think he had to keep a personal eye on her since the occasion of the beating she had suffered. He sat for hours in the waiting-room of the Police Department, smoking a pipe or sucking it like a child's dummy, and his brow would grow more and more thunderous until, when she finally appeared, he whisked her away with scarcely a word, driving the jeep with such a display of concentration that she didn't care to interrupt him.

At last, however, she was able to emerge and smile, saying, 'I've been told I can go.'

'Thank heaven!' was Marchmont's immediate response. Then he had the grace to ask, 'Does that mean anything has happened?'

'Yes. They've traced the two yachts which were berthed at the time of the kidnapping. A youth, who is studying English, noticed their names. One was *Sabrina* and the other *Prince Regent*. The *Prince Regent* had booked a berth in advance, but *Sabrina* came in, it was learned, because of engine trouble. Her skipper said he wasn't staying long and so the harbour-master hasn't an official record of her stay. In any case he says the vessel was referred to as *Konig Hal*, which is registered in Hamburg. If it *was* the *Konig Hal* then her name plates had been changed to *Sabrina*, of which there is no record in the Maritime Register. The student swears *Sabrina* was alongside *Prince Regent*, and I saw two yachts myself that day. The latter has been accounted for; she is on a cruise and has reported to the police in Casablanca. So now the search is on for the other one, under either or any name. I'm sure they'll catch the villains now.'

'Still, don't relax until you're far enough away from here,' Marchmont advised. 'Your particular fiend is right here in Tangier, remember.'

He proceeded to watch her like a mother hen until they were actually walking on to the plane in Tangier Airport, bound for Tunis. He had even troubled to ascertain that her room could not be reached from the street, and had Yussef keeping watch outside all through the night.

Their stay in the city of Tunis was brief because of time already lost. A visit to the Institut Pasteur, worthy remnant of former French occupation, was a must. Sally was wide-eyed as she went from department to department with Darien Marchmont tossing her scraps of information from time to time, for his conversation with the Director of the Institut was in French. Much research had been done into rabies and there was free vaccination against smallpox and other diseases.

Unfortunately the Institut did not control public health, its chief work was research, and Sally was distressed to observe much very real and horrible suffering and disfigurement when she accepted Marchmont's invitation to take a drink with him at an open-air café on the Avenue Jules Ferry.

It wasn't long before the first beggar arrived, a young, whining boy blinded by trachoma and limping on a club-foot.

'Empshi!' commanded Dr Marchmont.

Sally stared at him. His eyes were hard and his exclamation sharp and unkind. Her hand trembled as she sipped at her iced lime-juice.

Numbers two and three were even more pitiful to behold, a truncated man, dragging himself along on a rough wooden sledge and a small child with abdomen so distended, and limbs so stick-like, that he could have broken the civilised world's heart on a poster advertising famine relief.

This time Darien Marchmont's 'Empshi!' was even more severe. He said much more, which Sally did not understand, and the unhappy little procession dragged away through the dust and joined the blind boy in the shade of a wall some distance farther on. They were joined by others looking back at the café, and Sally felt a bitter anger on behalf of all human suffering.

'I would like to go to the hotel,' she said stiffly.

'Finish your drink,' he told her peremptorily.

Her eyes glared. 'Look here!' He obligingly looked, danger flashing from those steel eyes. 'You may order helpless beggars about, but you're not ordering me to do anything. I want to make that quite clear. Now I'm going back to the hotel.'

His arm reached out and gripped hers in a vice.

'You will sit where you are and *finish your drink*,' he told her in a voice straight out of a refrigerator. 'One way and another I've had quite enough trouble with you, and wandering about on your own you simply invite disaster. *I'm* not finished here yet, and you'll have the good manners to wait until I am. If this is ordering you about, I'm sorry, but I would prefer you think of it as asking.'

Her eyes on the grip of his restraining hand, where her own wrist showed white and bloodless, were expressive enough. He released her, apologised without humility, and she sat down again, her limbs feeling weak and watery from that head-on impact.

'If there is anything on your mind why don't you get it off?' he demanded.

She bit her lip without reply.

'I know what's bitten you. You want to take up cudgels for the halt and maimed and diseased. Well, you can't. There are too many of them. They're under one's feet and plucking at one's garments all along this damned, fly-infested, hellish coast!'

She looked, and could contain herself no longer.

'What a shame they should inconvenience you!' she

blazed. 'I'm surprised when you told them to go away you didn't use your boot.'

He looked at her and his lip curled.

'Pathetic, insular little Britisher!' he sneered. 'All pity and no relief. How typical!'

'At least I *have* pity,' she almost wept.

'And I do my poor best to supply the relief,' he told her quietly. 'I spent years learning their fiendish language so that I could communicate with the poor devils. I told them to go away and leave us in peace to enjoy our refreshment. I could see you were distressed, but I also told them I would see them when I had finished. There's quite a congregation of them, as you see. If you have any spare francs to add to mine I'll take them along.'

Silently she emptied her purse of loose change.

'Stay here,' he said quietly, and strode away.

She heard him talking to the tattered and deformed throng, even heard them laughing delightedly as he joked with them. They were attentive while he asked them questions and gave them advice, then he distributed the money and there were salaams and good wishes followed his tall, athletic figure back to the café.

'You wanted to leave,' he said to Sally. 'I'm ready when you are.'

She couldn't find her tongue on the walk back to the hotel where they were staying one more night; they had arrived at three o'clock in the morning, so were short of sleep. If she had spoken she would have wept, and did not want to lose face any more in front of this man. Once more she had been proved wrong about him and must eat humble pie. He was not unfeeling. He simply did not believe in scattering his emotions around for everyone to see, like her, for instance.

It was when she received a message from him, that he was having dinner served in his room and then retiring, that she decided the time had come to speak. She tapped on the door of his room, which was adjacent to her own, and entered when bidden to do so.

'I thought you were my dinner,' he said pleasantly, as though the afternoon had never been.

'I've come to say I was wrong to behave as I did,' she said quickly. 'You're right when you say people like me are insular and—and rather helpless. I took your point. I shouldn't have judged you hastily as I did. I don't know you very well and you are a—a—rather alarming person at times. I don't know what's come over me lately. I get so angry—especially with you, sir.'

'Yes,' he smiled ruefully. 'I had noticed. We appear to have a natural antipathy towards one another. But having knowledge of this thing may help us to guard against unnecessary explosions of personality in future. It's not very likely we will see each other again after this trip, so we must try to get along as best we can. Shall we shake on that?'

Arbitrarily she didn't particularly want to be endured for a given period and then forgotten, but she shook hands, smiled and said, 'Now it really *is* your dinner, sir. I'll leave you to enjoy it in peace.'

'Join me?' he invited.

'No, thank you,' she returned with an effort, for she felt he was only being polite, 'you must have had enough of me for one day. I'll see you in the morning then, sir. Six a.m.'

'Six a.m.,' he nodded, and closed the door after her with a sigh which she hoped was not of pure relief. Her ego was damaged sufficiently without having to admit she was anathema to the man. Over her own

lonely meal she found herself again making up doggerel rhymes about her new appointment.

> *I'm attached to Dr Marchmont,*
> *Much to the man's dismay,*
> *For every time we meet it's clear*
> *That I'm wished miles away.*
> *I'm attached to Dr Marchmont*
> *But we're scarcely ideal-matched,*
> *And if he had his way I'm sure*
> *I'd quickly be detached.*

She wrote this down, with many crossings out and
alterations, on the back of the menu card. She didn't
enjoy the meal; the couscous was rather too highly
spiced and the water-melon a little too watery; and the
strong black coffee—ugh! She decided to go to bed
early, too, with the prospect of an early start on the
morrow. For the first time she doubted her ability to
go through with the project ahead. Wasn't she, perhaps, a little too insular, a little too British? Such
people, even trained doctors who have worked in hospitals for tropical diseases, are really spoiled by their
soft way of living, by seeing a population over-
privileged and well fed, nourished on a National
Health Service which keeps them on their feet when
they are well and cossets them back to health when
they are not. How can such people suddenly have their
eyes opened to the under-privileged, the hungry, the
neglected, the hopeless creatures of earth without re-
coiling from the immensity of the job ahead?

'I'm committed,' Sally told herself uneasily as sleep
tried to close her eyes and doubt and fear wouldn't let
go. 'I must make the best job of it I can. I must follow
his lead, not let him down.'

Over the Mediterranean a storm broke and lightning rent an inky sky. Waves rolled, feet high, into the Gulf of Tunis and then the morning came with a smile on the shine of raindrops and an early freshness which belied the heat and humidity of the day to come.

The lorry was there outside the hotel on the stroke of six. It was a vast six-wheeler and its driver was a huge negro with a voice like the basso-profundo of an organ. His name was Hamed, which was Arabic in origin, but Darien Marchmont informed his colleague that Hamed was probably descended from South-Sudanese stock who had been originally brought over the desert, by raiding nomads, to be sold as slaves to the rich merchants of the Barbary Coast. A clerk, who was also expected to join the party, was ill with dysentery, however, so Dr Marchmont decided to leave without one.

'We'll have to keep a log between us,' he told Sally. 'I can't afford to wait around any longer. Hamed's also a mechanic and Yussef's handy with the radio; we pick up an orderly at Djerid, unless something's happened to him, too, so we'll push off after we've checked the load.'

Sally found herself with a list in her hand, fortunately typed in English, reading off items one by one. First there were medical supplies and drugs, then domestic items such as a butane-gas stove and two spare cylinders, ('Your department, miss,' as Darien Marchmont expressed it), a tent, several sleeping bags, tinned and dry foods, tanks of drinking water and one for keeping the radiator cool, and all the accumulated paraphernalia which helps to make life worth living in far away places.

Then personal luggage had to be stacked on somewhere.

'You're allowed three favourite books,' was Dr Marchmont's edict, 'and we can do a swop when we're tired of them.'

Sally took her mother's Bible, *A Passage to India* by E. M. Forster, of which she never tired, and a volume of Browning's poems. Her senior vetted her choice.

'You're allowed that as an extra,' he said, handing her the Bible. 'Take another.'

She finally, after much heart-searching, decided on a Graham Greene novel she hadn't yet read. Darien Marchmont told her he was taking volume one of Tolstoy's *War and Peace*, a travelogue 'by a johnny who crossed the Sahara west to east on his own' ... 'You never know, we might pick up a few tips before we've finished,' and Fitzerald's version of the *Rubá'iyát of Omar Khayyam*.

By seven they were ready to start and already the day was promising great heat.

Darien Marchmont finally looked his assistant over as though she was part of the truck. She was dressed for the first time in her jodhpurs and bush-shirt, her feet hot in woollen hose and brogues and her hair bleached almost white, by now, with tendrils stirring in the warm breeze from the sea.

'Don't forget your hat,' he reminded her. 'From now on you'll need it.'

'What about you, sir?' she asked. 'I haven't seen you wearing a hat.'

'I've got a sun-proof head,' he told her, 'born in India and continually exposed.'

'So that's why he sneered at the British,' she thought, as she climbed up into the cab where she was allowed the window-seat while Dr Marchmont sat in the middle. Yussef was wedged in a little nest behind the tail-board of the truck.

'And God bless all who sail in her,' was Darien's final merry wish as the truck lumbered down the hotel drive. Hamed laughed deeply, Yussef called 'Inshallah,' and they were off.

At first every village was interesting to Sally and all the hobbledehoy Tunisians interested in the truck, but there was no stopping and the miles sped by until the landscape was continuing monotony and hours passed without sight of human being or habitation. The land was green and moist, the humidity unpleasant. After three hours the party stopped for refreshment at a date plantation. Here there were people, merry and obviously well fed. They were tending the palm plantations, rows of trees like tall soldiers, and the greenish festoons of flowers, rather like the blossom of laburnum, would obviously turn into next Christmas's neatly boxed, sugar dates.

'If all the world could include dates in their diet,' observed Darien Marchmont, 'there wouldn't be many nutritional problems. A few dates, the heart of a lettuce and a piece of cheese make an ideal meal. We mostly eat too much.'

'I don't think I could work up much enthusiasm, or feel the urge to dress up, for such a banquet, sir,' Sally told him.

'Do you lead a busy social life, Dr Preston?'

'No. I haven't had time to for six years. Maybe I'll start after this spell of duty.'

She was drinking thirstily from a water bottle.

'You shouldn't do that,' Darien Marchmont told her.

'Why ever not? I was desperate for a drink.'

'You should discipline yourself to drink only in the evenings on trips such as this. You'll be a rag of perspiration again within the hour. I only tell you for your own good,' he added as her lips tightened in that now familiar way.

How it rankled, though, to be told something for one's good that one should well have known for oneself. Of course she perspired so that her second change of clothing that day (she had contrived to change while they were stopped at the date plantation) was soon so damp it was miserable to sit there being chafed round the waist and under arms by soaking seams; also her feet were wringing wet in woollen socks.

'Do I *have* to wear socks, sir?' she asked in desperation, at length. 'They're very uncomfortable.'

'I'm sorry, but you do,' he answered unequivocally. 'It's an uncomfortable trip for a raw recruit. I think I warned you.'

'Still,' her chin came out and she managed a tight little smile, 'if I see it through I won't be so raw in future, will I?'

He gave her a glance of grudging admiration, though he wasn't quite ready to voice it.

'You had better see it through,' he told her, 'because there's no turning back, and I don't want to have to account for yet another little hump in the desert.'

'Oh, there's no question of *that*,' she said confidently. 'I'm tough. You don't know how tough I am.'

He raised one eyebrow quizzically, so she added rather defiantly, 'One doesn't have to be big to be tough. Diamonds come in small parcels.'

His eyebrow descended and his lip curled instead.

'Let's not think of other things inclined to be diminutive,' he pleaded in amused tones, 'the microscope reveals quite a few I'm sure you'd rather not mention. I'm sure you're as tough as you say you are and if you are not nobody is going to hold you to account. Stop being so aggressive, my dear, uncomfortable young lady. I thought we had made a pact not to fight?'

She subsided, and when they pulled into Djerid, long after dark, she felt she never wanted to see the inside of that cab again in her lifetime, or its occupants. She was so uncomfortable, so hungry, so thirsty, so stiff and sore with sweat-soaked garments dried like cardboard on her back, so tired, without a hope of getting any sleep, and so out of humour that she stalked off to the house given over to their temporary use without a word for anybody.

When at last she was clean again, her newly washed hair swathed in a turban, she lay down on the bed allotted to her and tried to relax. It was bliss simply to be able to stretch one's limbs in all directions and she would have been content to stay there, forgotten by the world, for at least forty-eight hours.

When Darien Marchmont called, 'We eat in ten minutes, Dr Preston,' she didn't reply, hoping he would think she was asleep and leave her in peace. Hunger had left her, so had thirst and the desire for human companionship. It wasn't as though Dr Marchmont was a compatible companion and he was probably happy to be shot of her for a while.

Glowering in the open doorway he suddenly growled, 'Everybody's waiting. Didn't you hear me tell you?'

'I—I thought I might be excused,' she said faintly.

'Well, you may not,' he returned. 'This is the time we eat and drink and hold conference. I shall be obliged if, in future, you keep to recognised behaviour patterns without arguing every single toss. Now please make haste.'

She dressed, feeling rebellious, in one of the two cotton dresses she had brought with her. How she hated this Marchmont fellow to whom she was reputedly attached! He was continually rubbing her nose in the dirt, making her appear more awkward than she really was.

The dining-table was laid on a veranda where Darien Marchmont was chatting with three men, one in robes, the other two in European dress, but all with the pale-coffee countenances and hawk-like good looks of the North African Arab. They all stood, when Sally entered, and were introduced as Dr Ahmed ben Hassan, Professor Osman and Sheikh el Bashir. The two first-named had been lent by the United Arab Republic, under the directive of W.H.O. to make a field study of parasitic diseases in Southern Tunisia. They had quite a well-equipped laboratory and would be happy to show the newcomers round next day. Sheikh el Bashir had travelled for a day to meet Dr Marchmont and his party. There was an outbreak of sickness among the children of his tribe. Two had died. The Egyptians, he pointed contemptuously, were only interested in their little bottles and eyeglasses.

Thus were dismissed the cultures and microscopes of the pathologists.

Dr Hassan smiled deprecatingly and said in English, 'We asked him to bring us a specimen or even one of the ailing children.' He shrugged charmingly. 'What more can we do?'

'I think that's our job,' Darien Marchmont said quickly, knowing the Arab mind and his predilection for urbanity and creature comfort. 'We are equipped to go out and deal with the trouble.'

Both Dr Hassan and Professor Osman had come to dinner in opulent German cars. To find people living thus, on the fringe of the Sahara, was a great surprise

73

to Sally.

During the meal she was well and truly appraised by three pairs of sepia eyes, but it was the Sheikh who finally put their curiosity about her into words.

Darien Marchmont's voice wavered slightly as he interpreted for her benefit.

'Sheikh el Bashir compliments me on the great beauty of my woman, but regrets she is so puny. He wonders if, with correct feeding, you will grow.'

'I hope you put him right on the first point,' Sally said quickly, 'and tell him what I told you, that I'm tough.'

'Ah, yes.' The Arabic poured forth glibly from his brown throat. The Sheikh laughed appreciatively and clapped his hands in a kind of applauding salaam.

'What's so funny?' Sally demanded.

'I told him what you said about diamonds going in a small parcel. He liked that. He is going to tell it to his latest wife, who is also not as plump as he would like her to be. He thinks you are a great comic and marvels that you are also a doctor.'

'*Sughaiyar sitt hakim*,' murmured the sheikh.

'Little lady doctor,' Darien smilingly obliged.

'*Kaman hasan.*'

'Also very beautiful,' came the interpretation.

'I wish,' said Sally, her cheeks scarlet, 'you would tell him to shut up now.'

When the protracted meal was over and the Egyptians departed in their large cars, blaring their klaxons to shift occasional robed stragglers and stray dogs from their path, the Sheikh summoned a couple of his henchmen and three camels and rode off into the night.

'I've told him we'll be on our way tomorrow,' Dr Marchmont told his assistant, who was rising with difficulty from her chair. 'What's the matter? Are you saddle-sore?'

'I'm everything sore, but I'll get used to it.'

'Yes, well—we've covered the first three hundred miles. When the speedometer reads three thousand we should be nearing the end of our excursion.'

'Right,' commented Sally without flinching. 'May I go to bed now? Is—is everything discussed?'

'Just about. Here are the notes for today's log. After you've written them out you can turn in. I hope you have a very good night.'

Sally looked at him and said, 'Goodnight, sir.'

'*Sighaiyar sitt hakim*,' he murmured, and strolled off, chuckling, pipe between his teeth, to his own quarters.

CHAPTER SIX

At last she was working, and for this Sally was profoundly thankful. She hadn't thought to start the practical side of her work with W.H.O. at Sheikh el Bashir's village, if a conglomeration of habitations which could be folded up and silently stolen away could be termed a village, but at least there were people, some of whom were sick and all who could claim some minor medical attention, and so she was temporarily content and forgot her aches and pains and heat-rashes in the glory of doing the job she loved.

The party had been joined by a male orderly, who had had some nursing experience and could at least give injections adequately. There was a dearth of medical and nursing staff throughout the continent, Darien Marchmont told his junior. It would be decades before sufficient personnel had been trained to care for their own nationals. In the meantime international groups, such as their own, were making occasional forays into the hinterland to do what they could, which, he added modestly, was only a flea-bite compared with what was needed.

Jason, the newcomer, was almost blond and a Christian. Marchmont said he was a Berber and had obviously fallen under the influence of a French missionary. He spoke Arabic, Berber and French and was fond of joining in medical consultations between his seniors. The party was now complete, save for a clerk, and both doctors shared this chore which they cheerfully hated.

76

The first job was to examine the sick children. There were about two hundred people in the encampment and about twelve children were affected. They ranged in age from two years to twelve, and the older ones were less feverish and less seriously ill than the tots. It was two babies who had died, both males, which was the reason for everyone's great distress, especially the respective mothers. To lose a daughter was sad, but to lose a son was a positive tragedy. There was much petitioning to Allah not to take any more sons and the sick boys were getting far more attention than the girls, Sally observed.

'You're not here to westernise Islam,' Darien Marchmont told her when she mentioned this obvious injustice. 'You won't hear the women complaining.'

It was quickly obvious that the children were suffering from gastro-enteritis, fatal to young babies but less so to older children. Once the sufferers had been injected with antibiotics they quickly cheered up. One old man had gloomily asserted they suffered from the great 'belly sickness'. He remembered a cholera epidemic at the end of the last century which had decimated his tribe at the time.

While the doctoring was going on Darien Marchmont was patiently probing and questioning, finding out what physical troubles the tribe had suffered in the past few years, how many younger folk had died and how. Because Sally could not converse with her patients she felt she should at least volunteer to take notes. She wrote until her hand cramped and still struggled on, her penmanship becoming less and less legible. Dr Marchmont never appeared once to flag and she remembered that he had a reputation for running his assistants into the ground.

'I'll show him I, too, can keep going,' she determined. 'He'll expect me to crack, but I won't.'

The Sheikh, naturally, wished to return hospitality and invited the medical team to a feast that evening in his tent. Sally watched a large, rather moth-eaten sheep led out of the fold and tied to a stake. It had the innocent, bland expression of all sheep and only protested feebly when it was deftly turned on to its side by its small boy attendant, who proceeded to tie its legs together. Sally still didn't know quite what to expect and when a man shaved the wool from the creature's throat thought that she was witnessing a shearing. The knife suddenly struck into the bulging jugular vein, however, and as the blood ran into a shallow trough which had been dug the sheep's eyes glazed and a moment later the tethered limbs thrashed in rigor mortis.

Sally's next conscious moment was when she opened her eyes to behold Darien Marchmont's anxiously upon her. He shoved a glass of sal volatile at her. They were alone in the tent.

'Drink that,' he commanded. 'What are *you* starting?' he wanted to know.

'Starting, sir?' Her voice sounded far away in her own ears. 'Nothing.'

'Then why the big swoon? Am I working you too hard?'

She remembered.

'Oh, it was seeing the sheep—the poor sheep.' She held her head as she remembered. 'It wasn't the work, but I hated *that*.'

He gave a small, refined snort.

'How do you think mutton ever gets to your table, or beef, or pork, or chicken?'

'Well, *I* don't have to watch its disposal,' she returned, beginning to get familiarly angry.

'Honestly! I sometimes wonder how you got through your training. I suppose you handled your cadavers without turning a hair, but the sight of fresh animal blood makes a doddering idiot out of you. You, who are so *tough*.'

For the moment she couldn't help herself. She gave in to a primeval urge and struck hard. His cheek was blazing and her offending hand was in his, slowly being mangled.

There was an awful silence. Sally had never seen grey eyes blaze like beacons before, also the heat from him was somehow travelling up her arm and making her feel peculiar.

'You little shrew!' he said harshly, and bent his head to hers while she watched as though fascinated. Why she was convinced he was about to kiss her she didn't know, because suddenly she was lifted off her feet, turned over and soundly spanked where it hurt.

'Tit for tat,' he said, breathing hard. 'Do you want to start another round?'

'Oh, how I hate you!' she exploded. 'I suppose you bully that poor wife of yours. She must be glad you're far away at the moment. If you lay a finger on me again I—I—I'll——' She looked round for something either to break or throw at him, but the tent was lacking in portable items which could readily be squandered and she petered out rather like a damp squib.

Darien was to all intents and purposes himself again. He even had the audacity to smile.

'At least your colour has returned,' he said with professional interest and turned to leave the tent. 'I'll call you fifteen minutes before we eat,' he told her, 'and *be ready*. I want no sulks on top of your tantrums. One never offends one's desert host. Who knows when one may need his knowledge and his help?'

Sally wanted to weep when he had gone, but not entirely for the offence she felt had been committed against her person. She had been made aware of certain passions which had hitherto lain dormant within her, and these were vaguely terrifying. When she remembered that blazing face above her own, slowly and relentlessly descending, she had expected only one conclusion, a merging of lightnings, a fusion of alien personalities, a kissing and forgiving. It hadn't happened, however, and now she had to try to understand why her immediate reaction had been acute, personal disappointment.

The team spent a week in Sheikh el Bashir's encampment and saw all the small invalids back on their feet again. The water hole was examined and found to be reasonably clear as a source of infection.

'One must assume that these people have built up a certain immunity to most diarrhoeal troubles,' Darien Marchmont told his assistant casually—they were being very cool towards one another at the moment—'I think the enteritis came from fruit they admitting bringing in from the town. Do you agree?'

'Yes, I believe that is so,' Sally answered.

'Then put it in the log as our conclusion, Dr Preston. Everything goes into the log. If you ever disagree with me on any subject, that goes in, too. One of us is then eventually proved right. It's always rather fun waiting and seeing.'

Every day of those seven there was a doctors' round, as in hospital. The distinctive white-coated figures, followed by the orderly, went in and out of tents as though it was an everyday occurrence, taking blood pressures and pressing tender little abdomens and then enjoying jokes before moving on. There were two very old members of the tribe who also enjoyed a visit from the doctors. One claimed he had been born in the year of the great flood, which, if he was referring to the Nile overflowing its banks and drowning hundreds in their sleep, made him one hundred and twenty-five years old.

'Without a birth-certificate nobody's going to believe *that*,' said Darien. 'He was probably told about the great flood in his youth and has come to associate it with his earliest remembrance. I certainly think he's a centenarian, but by how many years I wouldn't like to say.'

The other senior member of the tribe was an old emaciated woman who was the doyen heading seven generations. She was about ninety-nine and had borne her first child at thirteen, who would now have been eighty-six. He had died last year. His daughter, aged seventy, was also deceased. Living were several great-grandchildren, the eldest of which was fifty-nine, who had a daughter of forty-four and a grandchild aged twenty-seven. This young man had a daughter aged eleven, named Halima, who was now recovering from gastro-enteritis. At thirteen, or perhaps a little later, she, too, would marry and bear children, maybe going off to a neighbouring tribe, for there was less feuding and fighting with one's neighbours than in former times and with intermarriage tribal health was much improved.

One of Sally's allotted tasks was to chronicle this amazing family history with Jason acting as interpreter. He translated the colloquial Arabic into school-room French for her benefit and she had to rack her brains to boil it all down into English. She took quite an interest in re-learning French and made a vow never to be content with only one language in future.

The last day at the encampment was particularly busy for doctors and staff. A middle-aged woman was dying of cancer, and this was too advanced for surgery or radium treatment to be of any use to her. In any case she would never have agreed to separation from her family. She had been suffering considerable pain for some time, but not since Dr Marchmont and his assistant had come on the scene. Twice a day the soothing needle, carrying its blessed burden of relief, had pierced the tortured flesh and given hours of peace. The suffering woman had rallied to call her family to her and give them her blessing; she particularly blessed her youngest daughter-in-law who was carrying the child which would take her place.

'I will live in him,' the woman told everyone. 'I will go and he will be born. It is written.'

Sally was worried about leaving the dying woman behind, for they could only inject morphia in person. To leave a dangerous drug behind in charge of in-experienced nomads was to invite trouble. A supply of codeine tablets might be left, with firm instructions, but these would not dull the pain as morphine could and sooner or later would have no effect whatsoever.

The woman was bright today, after her morning injection, and insisted on sitting up where she could watch the women about their day's work and the children playing.

Darien Marchmont came seeking his assistant.

'We're having a baby,' he said succinctly. 'The girl Jamila's in labour.'

Sally still wondered what all the excitement was about. Arab women had babies as naturally, and with as little fuss, as they ate. It was not for the W.H.O. team to interfere with natural functions unnecessarily.

'It's not her first, is it?' she now asked. 'Weren't there twins last year? Is anything wrong?'

'Apparently she has been struggling all night without saying a word. The husband was getting concerned. I've just had a look at her and the breech is presenting. I have her in our tent and Jason is boiling the instruments. Care to come along and be midwife?'

'Delighted,' said Sally. 'I haven't had a confinement since I did my maternity stint. I'll scrub up and join you.'

As water was scarce they had to make use of Dettol solution, which was rather harsh on the skin. Sally robed herself in a sterile gown and entered the tent which was closed to curious eyes and lit from power generated by the truck.

Jamila, whose name meant 'pretty', really lived up to her reputation. Her hair was pushed away under a turban and her large, dark eyes followed Sally's every movement. She wanted to know if her mother-in-law's pain was as bad as she was experiencing at this moment. Darien Marchmont told her that her mother-in-law was mercifully not in pain and that hers, too, would pass. The girl—she wasn't more than eighteen—sniffed eagerly at the anesthetic; they were using ether as being the least likely to create complications; and then the beautiful eyes glazed and when the lids were shut they remained closed.

Dr Marchmont put a pair of small red feet firmly in Sally's hands and manually dilated the cervix.

'I think the cord's round the neck,' he said, and grumbled, 'why doesn't she make a move?'

Just then the strong muscles in the girl's abdomen contracted and thrust, contracted and thrust again. Sally, who had small hands, slid them up to the baby's chest and then brought one tiny arm down—another.

'Good for you!' Marchmont almost snapped. 'Let's have more damned light, Jason! Get out of the way!'

The head slipped clear and the knot of the cord tightened round the throat.

'Easy does it.' The cord was loosened, but the baby

lay limp, not knowing it had been born.

Sally took charge of the mite when the cord had been cut and slapped and massaged, slapped and massaged, then placed her mouth to the tiny lips, looking so flaccid and fish-like and drew mucus, which she spat away before breathing in life-giving air.

The small heart fluttered under her hand and stopped again. She kept on, unrelenting, for half an hour, three-quarters, the mother opening large, soft eyes to behold the drama.

'Have I a son?' she asked Dr Marchmont, unable to keep silent any longer.

Darien Marchmont glanced across at his colleague.

'What is it?' he asked, and added grimly, 'or should it be *was* it?'

Just then a small scream split the air, followed by the sobbing sound of a new baby taking in its first air.

Sally, scarlet and triumphant, wrapped the creature in a towel and handed it to Jamila.

'*Thakar,*' she said happily, '*el wala ibn Jamila.*'

The young mother smiled indulgently. It *was* her son, her first son, for she had disgraced herself by bearing twin daughters last year. But a son was always known as the son of his father, not of his mother. This was the small Koko. Koko ibn Sherif, as he would be called. She wanted Sherif to know that she had borne him a son. He would be pleased with her and give her a gold anklet or a necklace of beads.

Sherif was brought into the tent and there were unashamed tears on his handsome, lean face.

'He says his mother has just died,' Marchmont told Sally. 'She said she was going to sleep, but now it is the sleep of death. I suppose we'd better go and make sure.'

In a way Sally was glad. All remembrance of pain was ironed out of the countenance of the dead woman, who must have passed away as her grandson was un-willingly entering the world. Perhaps their two souls had lingered for a loving chat, which would have accounted for the delay in the new one's arrival.

'By the way,' Darien Marchmont said later, Jamila and son having been transferred to the bosom of their family, 'you did a good job with young Koko. Well done!' She didn't know why this accolade should give her such pleasure, but it did. 'And I see you've been busy with the Arabic phrase-book. We'll make a lin-guist of you yet.'

'I doubt that very much,' Sally smiled, 'but I'm be-ginning to pick up the everyday phrases, the greetings and so forth. When old Bashir wishes me "*Salaam aleikum*", I now reply as you do, "*ma' essalaameh*". I don't know what it means, but it sounds good.'

'He fancies you, you know,' Darien observed, busily lighting his pipe.

'Who does?'

'Bashir fancies you. I know the signs. Don't be furi-ous, or faint, if he makes some proposal to you.'

Sally stared in horrified disbelief.

'You've got to be pulling my leg, sir.'

'No, I'm not. It's a supreme compliment, really, and you must turn him down tactfully, saying you are already promised elsewhere, or something equally con-vincing.'

'He must be fifty-five if he's a day,' Sally snorted, 'and anyway, I'm not a Moslem.'

'His passion would probably override such obvious deficiencies for a time.'

'You *are* joking?' Sally asked hopefully.

Darien Marchmont sucked in his cheeks, smiled but said no more on the subject.

That evening, just as she was about to turn in, Sally

became aware of a robed presence at her elbow, or rather two robed presences, to be exact. She stiffened, for Sheikh el Bashir was, for the first time in their acquaintance, fondling the flesh of her bare arm, almost pinching it. His son, Ibrahim, had attended a school in Benghazi and spoke some English. His role was that of interpreter.

'My father says you are very fair, Madam Doctor——'

'*Ya habibti*,' murmured the Sheikh.

'—and that he loves you. He would like you to share his tent, to stay with the tribe instead of leaving with the others.'

Sally was torn between hysterical screams and laughter. What would Tom say if he could know that her next proposal was to come from an Arab Sheikh? she wondered.

'I'm honoured to have won your father's regard,' she heard herself saying simply, 'but I have made a promise to travel across the desert doing my work as a doctor, and promises must be kept.'

Sally waited while Ibrahim translated. The Sheikh's eyes were inscrutable. Then he spoke again.

'My father says that such beauty is lost unless a good man possesses it. No one, he adds, bites into a pomegranate when it is withered and dry.'

'I hope to marry,' Sally answered. 'I am betrothed.' She added the man's name for good measure.

The Sheikh took his rejection like a man and asked that his admired one always remember him.

Sally staggered to her sleeping quarters, a corner of the main tent which had been sealed off for her use, but didn't get undressed. Later she heard Darien Marchmont preparing for bed.

'Dr Marchmont?' she called.

'Yes?'

'It—it happened as you said. Bashir proposed to me. At least, he asked me to share his tent.'

'Fair enough. Cut along. I'm broadminded.'

She came through the flap in the canvas.

'I don't happen to think it's funny.'

'No?' Darien had stripped off his shirt. His muscular shoulders shone in the light from the small paraffin lamp near his sleeping-bag. 'It's not a tragedy, either. Lots of women would give their ears to be paid a compliment like that. Sell the film rights. It'll make quite a story.'

'I happened to find it terribly embarrassing. Now had it been the son I might have considered the offer. Ibrahim's very charming.'

'D'you want me to tell him that?'

'Oh, no. No! Does the Sheikh know you're married?'

'No, I don't believe he could know that.'

'Which is just as well in the circumstances, because I told him I was going to marry you.'

There was another of those awful silences. Darien approached her, towered over her.

'You *what*?'

'Well, I was confused and I had to say something. Your name sort of just popped out.'

'You——!' he hauled his shirt on again, leaving her with a disturbing remembrance of firm masculine flesh. 'You absolute little fool! These people can smell a phoney a mile off. We've got to make it look good. Come on!'

He hauled her out into the open where a group of young men were sitting around a fire. He had put his arm about her and was hugging her close to his side, making her so suddenly aware of him that she could have screamed.

'Look as though you mean it,' he told her. 'They know Europeans demonstrate love openly. We're going to find a little hollow and they'll all think we're behaving like true European lovers.'

'I—I hate and despise you,' she quivered as he tugged her down beside him in a nook where rocks cut off sight of the encampment and only incredible stars peeped in on them from the black velvet that was the night sky.

'Well, I like that! I'm only playing up.'

'You're just trying to humiliate me. You have a perverted sense of humour.'

'I don't think I have a perverted anything. I'm a hundred per cent perfectly normal male showing superb self-control.'

'Ha, I like that! You haven't normal, decent feelings, let alone control of them.'

Suddenly her arm was in that vice again.

'Are you meaning to be provocativee, Dr Preston?'

'Let me go!' she demanded.

'So that you can slap me again? I warn you I shall retaliate.'

He released her hand and slap! it went, against the other cheek this time.

In a moment she lay pinioned, the breath crushed from her body and firm lips drawing her heart out of her very chest.

'Please!' she begged in the first gasp of her release.

He clamped down again and it was a long time before she could speak.

'What about your wife?' she whispered.

'Let's forget her,' he suggested, and when he sought her lips for the third time there was nothing stolen and nothing withheld. It was a splendid mutual effort.

CHAPTER SEVEN

AFTER another track south, the terrain growing ever more rocky and rising considerably, the W.H.O. party called on the Garrison Commander at Fort Saint. The C.O. was most helpful, being forthcoming on the subject of nomad tribes and their health. The fort M.O. held regular clinics, but nothing of an epidemic nature had occurred for a long time.

The truck was refuelled—this had been arranged with the fort in advance—and the water tanks replenished, and then the party nosed out in the direction of the least desirable and salubrious district of Libya, the Fezzan. The Colonel asked Dr Marchmont to look out for a Belgian couple who were attempting to cross the Sahara from the south in a Land-Rover.

'Zey will do zese sings,' he said in his attractive English, 'but zey are much overdue and I fear ze worst. Our planes have scanned zair planned route without success. Perhaps zey got a little off course, *hein*? You may pick up some news and use ze radio?'

'Certainly, Colonel,' nodded Darien, but gave a helpless gesture towards the wide blue yonder ahead, or rather the wide, hot, brown and yellow yonder, featureless, for one outcrop of rocks looks so much like another stretching out into infinity. 'It's a big place to be lost in.'

Darien now had a large map fastened to the roof of the cab. On it were marked a chain of oases stretching across the desert, each one marked clearly with latitudinal and longitudinal exactitude.

'Half a degree out and we would be like those Belgians, off course and overdue,' he said calmly.

That morning he had taught Sally to read a compass and take a bearing. They weren't speaking to one another unnecessarily today, which she found a relief. She didn't know how he was feeling about his behaviour of the previous night, but she was thoroughly ashamed and shocked at herself. He was a married man, and yet she had allowed herself to be magnetised by him into a situation where the ethics of human decency hadn't seemed terribly important compared with the urgency of momentary expediency and common delight.

How could she, Sara Jane Preston, have done such a thing? When he had said 'Let's forget her,' referring to his wife, she had allowed emotion to drown conscience, knowing full well that she was stealing and not caring terribly. She cared now, though. She felt belittled and horrified to know that there was a secret Sally, inside the earnest little doctor, who was the stuff of which 'the other woman' is made.

Of course she would watch her in future, this secret self, but wasn't really sure that she could control her. If there was another situation, contrived or otherwise, which placed her in the power of this spine-tingling man when he was in the mood to forget his marriage vows, just how strong could she expect to be? It had been such a strong feeling and she had been as helpless before it as a leaf tumbled in a stream or a house undermined by an earthquake. She was thankful he hadn't asked more of her. Dear heaven, she couldn't have argued with him if he had done.

She realised, now, that she had only just really grown up. Poor, sweet, undemanding Tom had been a schoolboy compared with this human dynamo sitting beside her and scanning the heat-hazed distance through binoculars. She wondered how many women actually went through life and bore their children without ever really plumbing the depths or ascending the heights of emotional experience. Perhaps they didn't want to know. She rather wished *she* didn't know, because now there was a yard-stick by which she would measure all her future male acquaintance. She didn't think there were many men in existence who could make her lower her standards for even one passion-filled incredible moment of eternity.

Hamed, who had bloodshot eyes by now, was sent into the back to rest with Jason and Yussef. Darien took the wheel of the great vehicle himself and Sally edged as far away from him as possible, almost hanging out of the canvas window-frame. She felt the binoculars thump on the seat beside her.

'You might keep a look out, Doctor,' Darien said quite curtly, and she wondered, with a little pain at her heart, if he hated her for what had taken place last night. 'We must reach the Hidwa oasis before night-fall.'

'I'm looking for the Land-Rover and the Belgians?' she asked dully.

'Anything,' he said. 'Nomads or camels or tents.'

An hour passed and her own eyes were feeling the strain of searching the blistering landscape but still she looked on, loth to confess to any weakness of which her companion didn't complain.

'Hold everything!' he suddenly exclaimed, slamming on the brakes. 'What's that at ten o'clock to my left?'

As the truck was fitted with a left-hand drive she looked out of the window aperture on his side, but could see nothing with the naked eye. She raised the binoculars and saw a distant, dim shape half buried in the sand.

'There *is* something,' she said hesitantly.

'Do you mind?' He took the binoculars and looked long and hard.

'I think we've found the Land-Rover,' he announced. 'Heaven knows what's in it.'

He decided the sand was too soft in parts to take the truck and called Yussef to accompany him.

'May I come?' Sally asked, jumping down, glad of a chance to stretch her legs.

'Get your hat,' he said, almost as though he disliked her. 'Don't let me have to tell you about that again.'

It was a longish walk and the sand was burning hot; so were the rocks where they were exposed. Now she knew why it was important to have good shoe leather and wool between one's skin and the molten surface. She was glad of her broad-brimmed hat, too. It made a little pool of shadow for her face and neck whereas her exposed forearms felt as though they were reaching into an oven. Yussef was wearing a species of *kaftan*, a turban-like headdress with a drape for the neck, but Darien Marchmont strode bareheaded, only protected by a thick, dark thatch of hair and eyes narrowed to the object of investigation ahead.

It *was* the Land-Rover, they discovered, but it was deserted. There was fuel in the tank and a spare can under the back seat. There was also a tank of drinking water and quite a goodly stock of dried and tinned food. There was also a change of clothing, a man's and a woman's, and an old French newspaper lying on the driving seat.

'This is it all right,' Darien Marchmont said thoughtfully, 'but where are the Mantelons? Why would they leave their vehicle where there is at least shelter, food and drink? Even if one loses a compass there is always the sun by day and the stars by night to steer a course by. They're not far off course, only about three-quarters of a degree.'

Sally said, 'Could they have been attacked by someone?'

Darien Marchmont pondered this.

'I doubt it. If nomads had attacked they would have pinched everything. That would have been the idea. But they're not murderous people and there are penalties to pay, even here, for breaking the law. There's a mystery here which I don't like.'

He and Yussef essayed two hundred yards in each direction, looking for clues, but to no avail.

'How long would the water keep?' Sally asked, turning the tap on the metal container and watching the droplets fall on to her shoe. It made her feel thirsty to watch them, but she had now schooled herself to drink only in the evening and perspired much less during the heat of the day.

'Indefinitely. It would have to be boiled, of course. Find a container of some sort, would you? We'll take a sample back with us and test it. There's not a lot we can do here. The Mantelons must have gone mental, I think, and wandered off. They could be anywhere, or what's left of them.'

He searched the sky with eyes like sharp needles, but there wasn't a wheeling kite or buzzard to give the game away.

Sally found a glass jar with dried peas in it, which she emptied into the glove compartment of the vehicle, loth to waste any of the carefully accumulated food even though none of it might ever be used. She then filled the jar with water and screwed on the metal top.

'That's done, sir,' she told him.

'Thank you!'

He regarded the water. It was faintly yellow, but this was not a land of crystal springs, so there was nothing unusual in that.

Next he took a compass bearing and carefully noted the position of the abandoned vehicle.

'We'll put that out on the blower tonight,' he decided. 'I suppose it's possible somebody else has picked the Mantelons up. Maybe one of them was ill and needed attention. We'll leave everything as it is just in case they're thinking of coming back, though I doubt it.'

A hot wind was now blowing particles of sand in gusts so that they stung exposed flesh.

'We've got to make up lost time,' Darien Marchmont decided, looking at his watch, 'so everybody get a move on.'

Sally took this to mean that she had almost to run to keep up with the longer strides of her companions. She felt like a rag as she climbed back into the truck. Hamed was again at the wheel smiling his toothy, negroid smile. Darien Marchmont said he was going behind for a spell and Sally decided he *was* human after all. He must actually be tired.

But when he knocked on the cab some three hundred kilometres later on it was to prove he had not been idle. He had been studying a map very carefully. He gave instructions to Hamed to change course slightly.

'I'm sorry if you joined this expedition with the idea of doctoring from nine till five,' he smiled at Sally. 'There's quite a lot of nothing between events, as you will now have concluded. North of the oasis where I plan to make camp there is a dried-up water hole; at

94

least it was dried up when my cartographer charted it. It's just possible the Mantelons were on a slightly northern route to ours and they may have found their water there. I hope you don't mind my Sherlock Holmes act keeping you from your dinner? We may be very late at Hidwa.'

Sally groaned inwardly but said no, she didn't mind. She wondered what he expected to find at the water hole. The Mantelons couldn't possibly have walked back that far, and why should they when they had a perfectly serviceable vehicle to drive in?

The water hole was advertised by a few hard-leaved shrubs and a single brown patch of brown grass on which lay a heap of bleached bones.

'A camel,' said Darien Marchmont as Sally shuddered.

There was no water to be seen, but the earth was soft in the crater and when a heel crumbled it there was even a little mud.

Hamed was put to work with a spade and soon there was a little yellow pit filled with ooze.

'There's water, all right,' said Darien, thoughtfully. 'But why did the camel die after he was watered? Was he just very old? And why didn't somebody drag his body clear? His head is actually in the crater.'

Sally was clearly getting tired of all the mystery and wanted to know what it was all about.

Darien Marchmont told her, while Jason was scooping some of the ooze into a phial for pathological experiment later.

'The Mantelons had everything to enable them to survive on that vehicle,' he explained, 'and yet something struck. Had they been able they would have left a note in the Land-Rover to explain their absence from it. I think they crawled away to die, somewhere

95

in the sand, and that we'll find the answer in the water they drank. They hadn't drunk much, if you noticed? I'm looking for typhoid, Dr Preston, and if I find it *we* may find ourselves with customers before we've gone much further, so contain yourself a little longer and keep your loins girded for action.'

Sally thought he could well be right. His delaying tactics had really been a carefully planned survey in search of a mortal enemy. It was akin to finding a needle in a haystack to find a source of contamination in a vast desert where the water holes and oases were marked with the importance of diamond mines in South Africa. But he had got his nose on the trail and he was not going to give up until he found something for his pains; his and everybody associated with him, she concluded wryly.

CHAPTER EIGHT

SOMETIMES Sally found herself wondering if she was really living a nomadic, occasionally hectic and exciting medical life, or if it was all a dream. She was amazed that life could exist at all in that vast desert, in temperatures which appeared to be rocketing with each day as July advanced, and yet there was abundant life in small communities, and this was an ethnological marvel to the young doctor in that some of the tribes had had very little truck with civilisation as it is known today and yet had built up a natural resistance to diseases which would floor white peoples: no doubt one 'flu germ could wipe these same people off the face of the earth, however, and therefore it was important to leave them not only to their chosen isolation but also uninfected by European-loving viruses.

Such a people revealed themselves at the Hidwa oasis, so called because it was shaped like a horseshoe. Sally had been rather disappointed in the oases she had seen so far. Sometimes the water was so far below ground that it didn't maintain either grass or tree and simply showed itself as a cairn of rocks on the apparently arid landscape. Hidwa, however, was all that an oasis is made out to be. It showed itself to the travellers at first in mirage, an inverted shimmering picture of palms and blue water ringed by green, coarse grass and suspended in the sky. It stayed thus for about half an hour, tantalisingly, and then the first palms appeared in their correct position and Yussef told his master, his nostrils twitching like a rabbit's, that he could smell water.

Sally didn't know what to think when three young horsemen approached the lorry, racing fine, mincing young stallions over the brown, stony earth with little regard for their hooves, brandishing rifles and yelling shrilly. She had seen that magnificent film, *Lawrence of Arabia*, but she hadn't quite believed this sort of thing really happened nowadays, and this wasn't even Arabia but supposedly peaceable Libya.

The lorry was stopped and Jason, who said the horsemen were Berbers who normally spent the summers on much higher terrain than this, descended to speak with them. He offered the information that the party were doctors—he contrived to include himself in this category to gain immediate respect—who gave their services free to the tribes because they were paid by the King to do so. It would have been difficult to explain the function of the World Health Organization in those immediate overtures, whereas even isolated tribes knew about the King.

In return the horsemen told Jason, whom they recognised as one of themselves by both his skin and his tongue, no matter how urbanised he had become, that they had been heading for Dhebel el Akhdar (the Green Mountains) when sickness had struck their people. They held their bellies to demonstrate the area of the sickness. Some had died, old people, mostly, and there were still about forty sick. They had struggled onwards, carrying the sick in relays, until they reached Hidwa where, because the water was good, they were staying until the pestilence had passed. Doctors were very welcome to share the water, but no one else, for it looked as though they might be there for some time and their animals also had to be grazed and watered.

This story was translated into Arabic for Darien Marchmont's benefit and then into English for Sally's.

'It looks as though we go to work again,' Darien commented as the horsemen went ahead with the news and the lorry trundled into action again.

There was a blessed pause for coffee—Jason supervised the making of it for the party, so as to be sure the water was boiled long and well—during which the elders of the tribe were in long consultation with the visitors about the epidemic which had stricken them. These old men remembered such an epidemic many years ago when doctors had come and stuck needles into those who were not sick. These had not caught the disease. Had the doctors such needles now?

Darien assured the elders that they had everything they needed in the truck, but first they must make sure what was really wrong with the sick people.

After that pause for breath the medical party knew no real peace again for days. After pathological tests it was fairly obvious that they had an epidemic of enteric (or typhoid) fever on their hands, but while they were waiting for the cultures to react they set about gathering the sick all together in one large tent, which was well sprayed with D.D.T. to deter flies and other pests. Berber blankets were then washed in a solution of chloride of lime and dried in the sun and set out in rows where the sick, all carefully washed and clothed in sterilized garments, were then lain. Already it was looking like a hospital, though it was a back-breaking business for the physicians to examine the patients, as they had no beds. The business of cleaning and disinfecting went on throughout the day while Darien Marchmont busied himself with pathology. He later announced that the trouble was definitely enteric fever; that it showed up in the blood samples of the sick and also in the specimen of ooze taken from the water hole north of Hidwa. The water from the Mantelons' tank was clear of infection, however. This made their abandonment of their vehicle even more mysterious.

'And in any case,' concluded Darien, 'one would think they had received the adequate inoculations before they attempted such a trip.'

An inoculation parade was held for the unaffected, after which Darien told Jason to ask if everybody in the encampment had now been accounted for, if those who were not sick had safely been inoculated.

A small child broke the silence after the question and was quickly cuffed for his pains. An elder said yes, everybody was now accounted for.

'What did the kid say?' Dr Marchmont asked the orderly, who was always on hand to act as interpreter.

'I'm sure it was nonsense, Doctor,' the fellow said disarmingly. 'He said there were two prisoners in a tent. I ask you? Two prisoners! That is small boy rubbish if you like.'

Darien Marchmont laughed too as he told the story to Sally, but she imagined that an uncomfortable silence had fallen over the crowd and they gave many a suspicious glance backward as they shuffled about their business.

'Could the child have been telling the truth, sir?' Sally asked, as they once again returned to the hospital tent.

'He probably was,' Darien Marchmont said promptly, 'because if he hadn't been everybody would have laughed and enjoyed the joke. I know these people, but they have to be handled with care. Whoever they have put away has offended them in some way and they wouldn't thank us for our interference. Did I tell you that entering field operations in this Service puts one in line for a job with the Diplomatic Corps? Leave it to me. Now this wee girl here is haemorrhaging. Did we get her blood grouping? A transfusion might help, but I haven't much hope of this one. You might get an apparatus fixed up, Doctor.'

They had to be nurses, doctors and night attendants, too; Darien even had to turn veterinary officer when a young stallion, the prized possession of a fifteen-year-old boy, decided to lie down and made no attempt to get up again, rolling in agony on the grass.

'I made it a colic ball and it's all right again,' he told Sally later. 'It was simply suffering from too rich a diet. Mainly its grazing has been short, brown stubble, on which these animals thrive, and here at the oasis the grass is too lush. If I had my way I would shoot all the animals—horses, sheep, goats, camels, donkeys, the lot. But a nomad without animals is like a city dweller without limbs. They are his food, his transport, his livelihood and his friends. When this business is over they'll merge into a happy unit once more and push off for the mountains where they really belong. Until that happy day the blighters are going to graze this place bare unless we can expedite things. Now I'm going to have a meeting with the elders and make some promises in return for information. In other words I want a showdown with them. Wish me luck.'

'Good luck, sir,' she said sincerely.

He turned to regard her.

'Thank you.' She felt a flush rising up her throat under that raking gaze which seemed to remind her that he had discovered she was also a woman. 'You're doing splendidly,' he told her. 'Keep it up, my likely lass.'

She felt tremendously pleased and encouraged by those words, and what else? Did she feel warm again where she had already decided to remain frozen and impassive? Well, she couldn't help her feelings. What she could do, and must, would be to control them at all times.

Sally had never seen a case of enteric fever before, but now she was seeing more than she had bargained for. She became familiar with the soupy green stools, the rash on the chest and abdomen, the enlarged mound of the spleen and the complication of jaundice. She had to supervise the disposal of excreta and see that the fit used the lime-pit which had been dug, instead of wandering off into the desert as heretofore. There were no new cases for four days and it began to look as though they were on top of the outbreak. Darien Marchmont operated on the young girl whose bowel had perforated, and even she was now holding her own. A radio message had been sent back to Djerid and the two pathologists working there. News of the outbreak would interest these specialists and it was up to them to get the wheels turning to disinfect the source of contamination.

Later the party at Hidwa were informed that Public Health Officials were being sent out from Alexandria in a W.H.O. helicopter to deal with the matter. They would also bring out supplies of drugs, dressings, fresh food and the mail.

Sally had wondered what it was she was vaguely missing, and now knew it was a daily post and newspaper. The two-way radio kept them in touch with Alexandria every evening, but reception was often bad and conversation was kept to the minimum. This was the reason Dr Marchmont now preferred to speak to Professor Osman and Dr Hassan at Djerid and relay news to Alexandria. It was a much more satisfactory arrangement and now that they were promised some action they were thankful the manoeuvre appeared to have paid off.

Sally was suddenly hungry for news of her father and Lucy, of her friends Cath and Jenny and Reba, who didn't even know of her new appointment. By reason of distance and absolute lack of outside news their doings suddenly had a tremendous interest for her and she was conscious of wellings of affection for them which assumed obsessional proportions with her.

'Dear old Jenny!' she would think in those moments before an exhausted sleep took her in thrall. 'I wonder if she ever got her Membership? It was so important to her that she did. She said she wouldn't marry Henry until she was his professional equal, which is a bit ridiculous when you think about it, but that was Jenny all over. Cath's baby must be born by now and I don't know what it is. Come to think of it, it would probably be born while I was in Tangier, and it didn't worry me unduly not knowing then. I'm even feeling interested in Tom again, wondering if he's missing me. Why is everything so important all at once? I think one has to have an emotional outlet and when it's impossible one creates an escape hatch for oneself. My friends and Tom are my escape hatch. Through them I escape into memory, which is all I've got.'

Her eyes, already glazing in sleep, suddenly shot wide open.

'Dr Preston, are you awake?'

'Yes, sir.'

'I've got news of the Mantelons. They're alive.'

'That's good! How? Where?'

'They're right here in camp. *They* are the prisoners. It's a bit dicey.'

Sally wriggled out of her sleeping-bag and unself-consciously put a cotton kimono over her blue pyjamas.

'How did you find out, sir?'

'By plugging away. I told the senior members of this outfit that if there was anybody in camp who had been overlooked they could well be carrying the disease, which would be a pity because we'd almost got it licked. I said nothing must delay their moving on because their livestock would be starving this time next week. I then casually mentioned that fodder would be dropped for the horses and camels, from the air, as a reward for any information they could give regarding a white man and woman who had apparently disappeared in the area from which the tribe had come. Then I had to lay on the flattery, saying how wise were these people and how they wouldn't have missed knowing about two white people in an area twice as large, and that I had been asked by the King to tell the white people, if they saw them, that he was hoping to see them alive and well very soon. I then went on to remind Bayar that his granddaughter would now live to bear sons for the tribe, thanks to me, thus putting him under an obligation.

'I sat back and waited, and eventually it all came out. As far as I can make out the Mantelons stopped when they were accosted (or so it looked) by these young gents on horseback, who can look so very terrifying. They (the Belgians) had watered at Hidwa and had then moved on to a camel-track off the main road, if such it can be called, which is why we found their vehicle off course. Already the Berbers were going down with enteric and the young men managed to convey that they wanted medicine. The Mantelons understood about the medicine, but refused to part with their supplies as they still had quite a way to go. That is when things became nasty, and finally both travellers *and* medicines were hustled off to the sick-camp under armed escort. The Mantelons did what they could, but they had only quinine in any quantity, which wasn't enough in itself to cure the fever. As the tribe pushed on to Hidwa, the Mantelons were pushed along, too, but they were allowed to move around freely until we arrived, then the elders considered we might think them rather naughty—they're crafty, the so-and-sos—and so gagged them and hid them away. The chief-elect told me that they were intending taking the couple back to their vehicle, and would never have made them leave it in the first place if only they had given the medicine without trouble. "We had sickness, *they* were well," was the argument they gave me.

'Well, the thing is, will the Mantelons be content to be allowed to leave and carry on as planned, or will they feel entitled to raise hell? I've promised their abductors fodder and forgiveness. The fodder is on its way, but the forgiveness is a different kettle of fish. Would you care to come along and meet the Mantelons and add your persuasions for a peaceable conclusion to mine? After all, no real harm has been done and these people were fighting for their lives.'

Fortunately the Belgian travellers were well and had been given food regularly. They spoke English quite well and were naturally furious at the treatment they had received and glad to get their feelings off their chest.

'We've been absolutely terrorised by those young ruffians,' Madame Mantelon said, 'and as we didn't understand their language, trying to communicate in mime was very difficult. We offered them money, but they laughed. We heard a vehicle arrive at the oasis, but they put a guard on us and we haven't had a moment's privacy, day or night, since. It's abominable!'

'There has been an outbreak of enteric fever here,' Darien explained, much to the Mantelons' horror, who had thought the trouble was dysentery, 'and so the tribe was desperate. They have great faith in European medicine and would probably have been content had you simply handed over your supply of drugs, whether they knew how to use them or not. You were right not to,' he added quickly, 'and as you went along with them you could at least supervise their use. Fortunately we came along and could take over, but as your inclusion in the party was not exactly of a voluntary nature, the tribe decided to keep it from us and return you, by stealth, to your vehicle. This is what they would have done,' Darien insisted, 'because they're not murderers and they have proved they are not thieves by not using armed force to take the drugs from you. Actually this is quite a wealthy tribe; their horses are superb, and not many tribes keep horses. These are a status symbol, as the Mercedes is over the Volkswagen. If you bring trouble upon them it will be difficult for parties such as ours ever to approach them. I am asking that you take into consideration their desperation in the circumstances and forget the whole thing, officially. You can write about your experiences in a light-hearted way, of course, but there was never any real danger to your lives.'

'I must uphold what Dr Marchmont has just said,' Sally said loyally, 'because they are a very gentle people at heart. Only the young bloods have rifles and they use them for hunting jackals and the like. They have lost fifteen dead in this outbreak and many more have been ill and are now recovering.'

The Mantelons at last began to smile again.

'It *was* a terrible experience,' Monsieur admitted, 'but I suppose it had its laughable side. Dori, on a camel, was the funniest sight I ever saw.'

'And yourself?' laughed Madame. 'You couldn't even stay on the brute they gave you, so you made the trip on a donkey. It was very, very amusing in parts.'

The chief-elect of the tribe, Bayar, was very glad to see the party of Europeans approaching him and apparently all in high good humour. They met as for the first time with much hand-shaking and touching of brows. In this happy atmosphere Bayar invited them all to the chief-making ceremony the very next evening. There would be a feast and dancing and merry-making. Jason was delighted to translate all this and accept for the party.

'So can we go to bed now?' Sally at last asked wearily.

'Do,' Darien told her. 'Tomorrow will be something you'll remember all your life.'

All but one of the invalids was mobile again and that one, Bayar's beloved and lovely granddaughter, had a memorable day, too, because her stitches were removed and her temperature kept to normal. This girl's legs and arms were mere sticks after her severe illness, but her large, luminous eyes were happy as she was told she would be able to watch the fun that evening. The womenfolk of the tribe, bracelets and earrings jingling, were busy from early morning preparing flat cakes of bread and sweetmeats. They had to cope with hordes of flies, but didn't seem to mind overmuch.

About noon two specks in the sky materialised as W.H.O. helicopters, and there was great excitement as they landed a little way from the oasis, raising blankets of dust and sand until the blades had ceased to rotate. Young men and horses whooped around these monsters as they disgorged bales of fodder; Bayar was smiling in supreme content that his co-operation with the white doctors had brought this blessing upon his tribe, little knowing that he would have received it in any case.

Yussef and Hamed, who had had the best of the past two weeks, were now busy carrying supplies to the unit, including fresh fruit and vegetables and vitamin pills. Sally seized hungrily upon her bag of mail and actually found herself with a spare hour to read much of it. She had a favourite spot by the water where she could hear it tinkling from far underground. This was probably a subterranean river with a source up in the Atlas mountains.

Letters from home came first; her father wrote that he was very happy and Lucy was enjoying 'messing about' with housekeeping. She was starting going on the rounds with him and would be taking over Robbins' surgery next week. The dogs were fit but obviously missing her.

'So am I,' he concluded. 'I may have a new wife, but I still have a niche for my beautiful daughter.'

'Dear old Daddy!' Sally murmured, her eyes moist.

Lucy's letter was full of strange and weird domestic experiences; the first cake which had fallen as flat as a biscuit, '—and Norman thought that's what it was meant to be and praised me for it.' The mysteries of the automatic timer on the electric cooker on the house-keeper's day off. 'I set it for seven o'clock and thought there had been a power cut. I had to open a tin of pilchards which brought Norman out in a rash—I didn't know about his allergy to tinned fish until then and he hoped he might have outgrown it. Next morning out of the depths of sleep we were awakened to a shriek from the cooker which announced that the roast

lamb and baked potatoes were ready for our delectation. Apparently I hadn't realised the fact that the
darn thing works from a twenty-four-hour clock——!'

Sally chuckled and then froze as she became aware
of Darien Marchmont nearby. He had this effect on
her at all times when they were not working together,
as though he was equipped with radar which pierced
her physical consciousness ahead of him.

He pushed a couple of bananas into her hand.

'Here, you need these. Otherwise those pretty teeth
may drop out.'

'What a horrible thought!' she grinned, and added,
'Sir,' for good measure.

'Call me Darien,' he invited, and smiled airily. 'I
shall call you Sara,' he nodded. 'I think it's a pretty
name and we're off duty at the moment. After all,
we've come through a lot together.'

'Very well, Darien,' she tried it out experimentally,
peeling the first banana and biting into it with relish.

'Much from home?' he asked, nodding at the mail
beside her.

'Quite a bit,' she told him. 'It seems to mean more
hearing from everybody out here. Did you hear from
your wife?'

'No, as a matter of fact I didn't.'

He stared ahead deliberately awaiting her com-
ments.

'I expect she—she missed the post or something.'

'I never hear from my wife on these trips.'

She look startled. Was he sad, bitter or what?

'Perhaps you have an understanding,' she suggested.
'Everybody can't communicate by letter.'

'I long to hear from her with all my heart,' he said
passionately. 'If only I had a wife who would write to
me! Even if it was only a postcard now and again, tell-

ing me of some stupid hat she had bought. Sara, I'm a lonely and desperate man.'

She looked at him in some alarm.

'I thought you were a controlled and disciplined person, sir—Darien. You hide your true feelings very well. I'm sure if your wife really understood she would write. She can't know how you feel at these times.'

He stared into the water, then rose and walked away without another word.

What sort of wife was she, Sally thought indignantly, who could neglect her husband so, working as he worked with a sense of dedication both admirable and rare? She must be a flighty piece. She had appeared rather petulant on that occasion in the foyer of El Minzah. Maybe he loved her whereas she merely accepted this as her due.

Sally read on, but her mind now kept returning to Darien Marchmont and his marital problems. Supposing that woman went too far and there came a day when he didn't mind not receiving the letters which were his due? What might happen then? He was an attractive man, as she knew to her cost, and other women might be only too glad to know he was looking around again.

'If I had a husband like Darien I would keep him,' Sally thought fiercely. 'I know he can be hateful, but that's just the other end of the scale, and I'm sure he would be the tenderest and most satisfying of lovers. But to see him so lonely and desperate—that's bad. It makes a woman want to help if she can, and when I wasn't even trying things were bad enough. I really mustn't become involved, except as a confidante. Now I suppose I'd better get back to work. I see he's on the job again.'

CHAPTER NINE

THE chief-making ceremony was colourful and exciting, also it was extremely noisy and soon Sally's head began to throb. There had been the usual feast to start with; whole sheep were roasted, though on this occasion Sally had taken care not to witness the butchery. Stringy mutton reared on dry stubble cannot produce the luscious lamb with green peas of which the British are so fond, however, and Sally made a pretence of feasting, taking only as much food as would not offend her hosts. She drank sparingly, too, of a species of date wine which was extremely potent.

After the feasting the young men held a few horse-races, raising the sand into a yellow cloud which settled over the remains of the food, and then, as darkness fell, the fire burning in the midst of the encampment was stoked so that there was a pool of brilliance in which wrestling matches were held and into which the girls, dressed in their prettiest and all a-jingle with baubles, bangles and beads, danced and swayed until they had hypnotised themselves and everybody else into a state of somnolence.

'Have you liked it?' Darien Marchmont asked his colleague, coming to sit beside her for the first time that evening. He had deferred to his hosts by staying with the men during the actual ceremonies, but now only the children were attempting to emulate their elders and dance or wrestle as their inclination might be. It was after midnight, and a crescent moon lolled back and smiled benignly on the scene of human activity, or rather inactivity, for many of the celebrants were now 'sleeping it off' while the new chief, Bayar, was snoring vociferously in an upright, chieftain-like position.

'It's been like something in Cinemascope,' Sally said. 'I can't quite believe it.'

'I told you tonight would be memorable,' Darien reminded her. '*Ayh maluk?*' he asked with a slight frown.

She had heard him ask the men this question often. She now knew it meant, 'What's the matter?' or 'What's up?'

'A bit of a headache,' she admitted. 'I suppose I'd better go to bed.'

'No, don't do that,' he said quickly. 'Let's stretch our legs first. Now that the dust has had time to settle the air should be worth breathing. There's nothing quite like desert air at night. Somebody should bottle it and sell it for wine.'

He sniffed appreciatively as they wandered upwind of the camel-lines. Some of these beasts gave vent to their typical disagreeable moan of complaint and allowed their silken-fringed, heavy lashes to droop again as the disturbance passed.

'They scare me,' Sally said frankly. 'I think it must be the pitying arrogance they seem to possess.'

'Which comes from knowing the hundredth name of Allah,' he explained. 'Nobody else knows it, and who's going to get a camel to tell?'

As Sally's eyes looked up at him in true enquiry he seized her hand and squeezed it.

'You must have been a beautiful child, Sara. I'll bet you believed in everything until you simply had to be enlightened for your own good.'

Her fingers wriggled like tadpoles in his grasp.

'Of course I believed, and still do believe in many things. I simply transferred my fantasies into facts. For instance, I believe you would like to be holding your wife's hand rather than mine and that you shouldn't use mine as a substitute. Would you let me go, please, Darien?'

'I don't want to lose you down a hole,' he said, allowing her to slip away.

She knew he couldn't have created a hole, but the very next minute her right leg disappeared into nothingness and her mouth was full of sand.

'Are you all right?' He was half laughing as he knelt and hauled her to him, dusting sand out of her eyes and riffling his fingers through her hair to clear it. 'Most of this terrain is still rock, but occasionally there's a small valley filled with pure sand which will bear little weight. You just found one. Now perhaps you won't object to my holding your tiny hand in mine?'

He seized her fingers and gripped them hard, somehow sending a message by electrical impulses to her somewhat stunned brain. She had been hesitating on the point of tears from the shock of feeling the ground sink away beneath her feet and also from a vague unease her companion's unprofessional presence always wrought in her. Now she found herself channelling this emotion into the beseeching of her eyes as she looked up, a long way, into his. He reached down without a word and took her lips, tenderly, strongly, drawing from her the little strength she had left, so that she leaned against him, and the small fire they had ignited in a kiss became a blazing furnace of desire all in a moment, almost out of control so that the stars, the moon were quenched in the unreasoning demands of physical passion.

From a long way off came Darien's voice, uncertainly: 'Sara, I think you should know——'

The fact that he could still speak, whereas she had temporarily become disembodied emotion, gave her back her sanity. She pushed him away from her and stood panting, ashamed and afraid.

'I think you're missing your wife, Darien——'

'No, actually I'm not.'

'Please let me speak. I'm very sorry for what just happened. I suppose I encouraged you to behave as you did, but now I know what can—can happen I'll be careful in future. I'm a single person and I suppose I am, subconsciously, looking for romance, but I don't want to find it with a married man, as you will understand; not even a married man having domestic difficulties.'

'May I——?'

'No. Please let me go on. I think there's a certain amount of physical accord between us; but as we're two Europeans in a vast desert, thrown together almost twenty-four hours a day, I suppose that's hardly surprising. When we met in Tangier and there were distractions, this accord was not exactly obvious. I want to apologise for being momentarily weak. I wished you to do what you did, and now I'm sorry.'

'So am I, that I have apparently disappointed you.'

Sensing offended masculine ego, she said rather sharply, 'There's no question of disappointment. You must know you're attractive to women, Darien.'

'You would have me think only to other women.'

'I find you very attractive,' she said patiently, as though to a rather obstreperous child, 'which is my main reason for calling a halt to things between us here and now. At Sheikh el Bashir's camp we played with fire, but it was only play. Tonight was deadly serious, and if you feel no sense of responsibility towards others—I do.'

She turned to walk away and his voice came after her, challengingly.

'Walk carefully, Sara. Walk very carefully on unfamiliar ground.'

She knew he was neither referring to the terrain nor her recent fall.

She was approaching the camp again now. A curl of smoke still rose from the dying fire and the sheet of water lay like opaque glass under the moon, subterranean streams making strange bell-like noises from far below: the fringing palms were absurd, inverted feather dusters sweeping the sky. It was a scene set for lovers, and yet there must be no love—it would be wrong.

A mosquito bit hard into Sally's neck and she slapped at it angrily and impatiently.

'There's always something rotten in apparent perfection,' she said testily. 'I wonder why there have to be pests?'

'Or disease or malformities,' said Darien from behind her. 'Actually you're seeing a few pests too many, my dear girl. Things are not what they seem. How much of our mad moment was due to the fact that it would appear to be stolen fruit? If I told you I wasn't married, had never been married, would it make any difference?'

She stopped in her tracks, once more rigid with shock.

'Are you joking again?' she asked in a small, trembling voice.

'I never joke about really important things,' he said

sharply. 'Please get it out of your head once and for all that I am either a persistent funster or suffering wifely neglect. The only Mrs Marchmont in my life is my dear old witch of a mama who would revel in the situation we've contrived here. The lady to whom I believe you imagine I'm bound, who spent some time as my guest in Tangier, is Serena Danely, attractive widow of an erstwhile friend of mine. George and I were both suitors for Serena's hand at one time, but I'm convinced the lady made a wise choice, though she is very fond of me still and I of her. I find it easy to relax in her company, as she is extremely decorative, and we have a common interest in her small son whose godfather I am. Maybe Serena and I would have one day—who knows? But the chips are still on the table and the wheel is not yet still. I fostered your idea that I was married because I thought it would make you feel safer, when my company was forced on you a long way from home, to have a "wife" safely in the background. I know you must have thought me a heel often. Sometimes I only had to look at you to forget my role, and I had no thought of any wife a few minutes ago. There was only you, Sara, and me and this thing between us. Was it only a bubble, or——?'

Once again he had come dangerously close, and she felt like a spark which hovers, knowing it must fall back into the brightness of the fire which gave it birth. She trembled and knew she was not only affected by his physical presence but also afraid of the freedom of choice now offered her. She was relieved to find she could feel angry.

'I think you've behaved atrociously,' she said coldly. 'You knew what I thought and you led me on to betray the principles by which I have always lived. I lowered my standards, and for that I can never forgive myself or you. I suppose when you put on that show for El Bashir you didn't think how it might affect me? How I might be attracted to you and torture myself with the thought? I've been afraid to be alone with you, not knowing how far I could trust myself. Your confession has come a little late, Dr Marchmont. Our stolen moments of delight had their being in guilt, as far as I was concerned, and you can't suddenly make a statement and give me back my innocence. I don't know what you're offering, whether it's eventual marriage or a dalliance across this very large desert. I don't want to know, because I've made up my mind to come to my senses and get over this stupid infatuation. I'm sure we're both being very near-sighted about this. There simply isn't anyone else in the picture. I suppose I'm quite an ingénue in matters of the heart and you are a man of the world. You say you aren't laughing now, but you will when you see Mrs Danely and tell her about all this. I'm sure she will enjoy it, and do tell your mother if she would be interested!'

'Sara,' he murmured unhappily.

'I'm going to bed now,' she concluded, 'so I'll say goodnight. I expect I'll be laughing by morning.'

What remained of the night was a misery for young Dr Preston, however, and when Yussef brought her a mug of tea she was grateful to think it lay behind her. From now on things could only get better. One did get over unfortunate attachments in time, and she had now convinced herself that any association she might have with Darien Marchmont, apart from her professional appointment, could only be classed as unfortunate. A man with power like that over a woman was dangerous, as well to be avoided as an iceberg in mid-ocean.

What she didn't admit to herself was that she was in reality seeking a safe harbour from those same deep waters. She had been afraid of falling in love, of committing herself beyond the point of no return. She fondly hoped that she had stepped back in time. But if so what was this nagging ache in her bosom whenever she remembered the sweetness that had been without discipline, the compulsion which had not answered to either curb or rein?

She dressed for the day ahead. Thank heaven for work! Yussef returned with a letter addressed to her in her senior's sprawling, careless hand which she had now learned to decipher with comparative ease. She deliberately bade her heart, which thrilled at the sight even of his script, sternly to be still.

'Dear Dr Preston,' it began formally, 'While you are still asleep'—have I been asleep? she asked herself—'Hamed and I are taking the Mantelons to rejoin their vehicle and see them on true course to their rendezvous at Fort Saint. The officials have been notified of the couple's safety, but naturally they want to finish the expedition they began. They wish to convey their sincere regards to you but would not have you disturbed. I hope you can cope with the hospital unit in my absence; I expect to be back by nightfall, but who can tell?

> 'El hamdulillah,
>
> Marchmont.'

She told herself she was glad that he had the good sense to keep the missive short and businesslike. It would have been unforgivable to refer to last night through the media of pen, ink and paper. Yet couldn't he have added a postscript, she asked herself arbitrarily, telling her how sorry he was for having angered her?

Perhaps he wasn't conscious of having angered her, she argued. Maybe he really loved her and she was being unnecessarily prudish and cruel in her denial of him.

'But he never mentioned love,' she almost cried out. 'I really didn't give him the chance to,' she had to admit, and found her eyes, like defiant children, roving the camp scene, longing to see him about his business while knowing he was many miles distant.

It was a quiet day in the camp. More fodder was dropped from the air and the oddments of mail which had accumulated since the last time. The Berbers were obviously beginning to fidget to move on; they did not relish the great heat of the desert and would not have been here in August had it not been for the epidemic which had stricken their numbers. Already they had been delayed by the illness and death of their chief a couple of months previously, and then by their meetings and consultations while they elected a new chief.

Bayar came to ask Sally how long the sick would be before they could travel, but as their common interpreter was absent she had to give her answer in dubious French to Jason, who passed it on. Possibly two weeks, she said, but the orderly interpreted this as two days and the new chief left looking highly delighted and rubbing his hands.

There was a birth that day, but this time it was an easy and straightforward one. Only the mother's disappointment that the scrap was a girl spoilt the event for Sally, who thought she had rarely seen such a beautiful baby.

'Jamila,' the doctor crooned over the mite, giving it her own welcome. 'You lovely little Jamila.'

'Huh!' was the mother's response to this, in her own tongue. 'That one is no Jamila. Too small, like a baby monkey. Girls should be big and strong for bearing sons for their husbands. Her name will be Safa.'

Later on in the day nature took her course and the newcomer was clasped to its mother's breast. The older women had remarked that it was a small child but well proportioned and looked healthy enough to bear many children.

This preoccupation with bearing children Sally found rather distasteful. In a community where women were still chattels there was this man and boy worship which offended her European mind. The men and boys even took their food first and were regarded as superior beings. Even while Bayar's granddaughter had been very ill there was some grumbling among the men patients that she received treatment before they did. It was all rather absurd to the forthright Sally, but Darien Marchmont observed at such times: 'These are a part of the twain we will never quite meet. Doctor 'em and move on. We can't alter 'em.'

She had a chance to sort the small bag of mail earlier than she had anticipated and put aside three letters for Dr Marchmont. One was meticulously addressed and bore traces of perfume. It had the sender's name and address clearly on the back.

Mrs Serena Danely, apparently enjoying the cool, hill air of a villa in the Auvergne district of Southern France at the time of writing.

Sally imagined the 'Villa du Lac' with unconscious longing. It would be long, low and white with a very red roof and decorative brickwork round all the windows which would be fitted with striped awnings in green and white with deep fringes. The lake would be mountain cool and the rich would sail their yachts on it, but in the grounds of the villa would be a swimming-pool, heated to tepidity at this time of year.

Sally felt suddenly hot and uncomfortable; her hair was full of sand particles and her woollen hose almost squelched in her sensible shoes. Why was she doing this? What was she getting out of it? Experience? Yes. Frustration? Doubly yes. Satisfaction? Only occasionally. But would she like to go back to the Hospital for Tropical Diseases, with its white beds and wards kept heated (or cooled) to a steady seventy degrees fahrenheit winter and summer, with regular hours and a decent bed to sleep in and all the amenities of an advanced civilisation awaiting those times one was off duty?

At the moment the grass was greener on the other side of the fence, and she knew it. She had romped in those same green pastures and been bored almost to tears at times. At least she hadn't been bored on this job; it had been almost too interesting at times for comfort.

That jingle came back into her head in a different form:

> *I'm attached to Dr Marchmont*
> *in a very personal way,*
> *And life's dead and dull without him*
> *Which is all I'm going to say.*

'Pull your socks up,' she told herself sternly. 'You put all that nonsense away from you last night, very right and properly.'

She was amazed to find a letter from Tom in her own mail. Her heart lurched with shock and she wished she didn't have to open it. How had he got hold of her address, and why had he decided to break the ban on their meeting or communicating in future?

To open the letter was the best way to find out, and this she did, at length, sitting by the water's edge to read, pestered by flies and feeling wholly uneasy.

'My dear old Sally——' that makes me feel a hundred for a start, she decided. 'I know you said no letters, and I have tried to respect your wishes, but I hope you will forgive this intrusion because we *were* engaged, and that makes you closer to me than any other person of my acquaintance since Mother died. Things have been happening to me, as they seem to have been happening to you; Lucy gave me your address and it appears you did get the job you wanted with W.H.O. I'm so glad for you and hope you're happy. I was astonished to hear about your father and Lucy. I'm not surprised you wanted to get away from a set-up like that, which must be intolerable. Well, the crux of this letter is that I want to see you, Sal. I *must* see you. I was very fond of you and there is something I have to discuss with you which may affect my whole career. I have the whole of September for my annual leave and perhaps I may fly out somewhere to see you. Anywhere would do. You name it and I'll be there. If you simply can't bear the idea of seeing me again tell me to buzz off and I'll understand that your interest in me and my affairs is now null and void.

'With sincere regards,
Tom.'

Sally read the letter again with a feeling of irritation. How like Tom to hint at so much without actually saying anything. Things had been happening to him. What things? Had he a different job or fresh digs, or had he even had a raise in his salary? Why should he want so desperately to see her when he had scarcely raised any protest about her slipping away out of his life? Why must he involve her again when she felt like someone on another planet? He reminded her that they had been engaged yet didn't mention the word love. He had been 'very fond' of her, was the best he could do, which put her on the same level as a favourite sister or even a benign aunt.

'I suppose I *had* better see him and get whatever it is over with,' she decided, and wondered what she would say if Tom wished to revive their relationship.

Water after wine? That she couldn't accept even though the wine had soured after the first heady cup.

She remembered reading a poem a long time ago, in her impressionable youth, which had pierced beyond her emotional experience. It must be glorious, she had pondered, to be loved and love in such an ecstasy of pain. And yet wasn't something of the sort happening to her now? Hadn't those same verses been written for her and Darien?

She remembered the poem suddenly and vividly. It was called 'Wines', though she had forgotten the name of the poet who had never known fame.

> *I have drunk deeply of vintage old and new*
> *And found that sense*
> *The most responsive was to rich, intense,*
> *Warm-blooded, liquid fire, and knew*
> *That drunken, Heav'n was very near*
> *—And you.*

(Oh, Darien, I must have been drunk when I wanted you so! There was madness in the touch of your lips and all I want to know of Heaven in your arms.)

Oh set me down, sweet fate, upon a tavern floor,
And let me see across the ruby glow
The warmth of friendly eyes that know
My weakness and my greatness, and adore,
With me, the distant background of a song
  For evermore.

And waking in the morning, why then weep?
And is my love but of an hour,
And did our glasses kiss but to turn sour
Untasted? Give me sleep, a drunken sleep,
And waking—wine—more wine—
  Drink deep.

Oh, thou, who art my cup of bitterness
So full, raise now they acid lip to mine,
That I may drink strange sweet—not sweet
  the less—
Of love remembered in as stale a wine.

A dust cloud in the distance revealed itself as the truck and Sally leapt up and grew excited in the prospect. Well, she was glad to see Hamed and Dr Marchmont back safely, wasn't she? That was really all. There wasn't anything more because wine went stale, as the poem said. Last night's sweet kiss was today's rather bitter remembrance.

Still, her smile was without rancour as she greeted the travellers, the dust of the desert like pancake make-up on their faces. While Yussef scurried to brew up refreshing *shai* she smiled brightly and said, 'You must have had a tiring day, sir. It's been quiet here and I've written up the log. You must get to bed early. There's nothing to worry about. There's some mail on your locker.'

His tired, strained eyes raked her over as though she was something new to his sight.

'Well, thank you, Dr Preston. I knew you could cope.'

She felt a welling of friendliness towards him. It would be pleasant if they could be friends instead of the other thing. And yet would it? Did she want Darien Marchmont's friendship after that phoenix pyre from which she had retreated with charred wings?

'The trouble is I don't know what I want,' she mused as she ambled in and out of the hospital tent making sure all was well for the night. 'I have to stop being emotional and try to see things clearly.'

But now that Darien was back, that she could see him, the foolish delight she felt was neither practical nor sensible. She decided to let this foolishness ride until it fell heavily and was no more.

CHAPTER TEN

DARIEN did not attempt to offend her again, for which she should have been more relieved than she was, and made no reference to the business on the night of the chief-making apart from saying once, as he came up behind her and she jumped in alarm, 'Don't do that. You're really quite safe from me. The red flag went up, if you remember? We seem to be getting our house in order here and I intend to push north, where we could both do with a spot of leave, I feel sure. On the return trip we'll follow the coast more or less, so it won't seem such hard work. There'll be good roads, for one thing, which the Italians built. These attract their own communities, which pop up like rabbits out of warrens and are about as hygienic.'

'A spot of leave will be very acceptable, sir,' she said enthusiastically. 'I know it isn't really very long, but it seems an age since we left Tangier.'

'I know,' he agreed. 'One has to do something when left to one's own resources and so one usually works twice as hard. It tells in time. Also this is a tough life in these temperatures. It's no job for a woman.'

'Have I—failed you, then, sir?' she asked.

'No. You've risen to the occasion extremely well. But you've lost weight and your natural colour has gone. I don't want to drive you into the ground. As soon as we're free of this lot we'll head for the sea and you can put on that pretty little blue two-piece again and swim to your heart's content.'

'Where will the sea be, sir?'

'Off Benghazi. That's a dirty, adorable little place, if you don't know it. It has a certain friendliness and charm which persuaded me to have a villa built overlooking the beach. You are very welcome to stay in my villa, of course, Dr Preston.'

She bit her lip and said, 'Thank you, but I think I'd better stay in a hotel.'

'It's a large villa, and it has a very nice swimming-pool for when the sea is not amenable . . .'

'Still, sir, if you don't mind . . .' She was thinking of Tom who would be flying out to discuss those important matters of which he had hinted. One could scarcely encumber one's host with one's friends.

'Very well, Dr Preston,' he said, rising. 'I'll see you're booked in at the Vienna. That's a very good place, run by Europeans.'

He didn't sound hurt, he didn't sound anything, and yet she felt a glacier reared between them.

'As soon as it's possible to send a cable, I would like to do so,' she told him.

'If you will write the substance of your message I can see it goes out on the radio for you,' he said helpfully. 'I have a cable to send myself.'

When she had learned the approximate date of their arrival in Benghazi, about ten days hence, she handed over to Dr Marchmont the message bidding Tom meet her at the Vienna Hotel. He read it in silence and then observed, 'In that case I'd better book you two rooms. Perhaps you and Dr Rydale would at least join Serena and me at the Villa Inshallah for dinner one evening?'

She felt she couldn't refuse anything else, though she really had no desire to see Mrs Danely again.

'Thank you, sir. That would be very nice.'

He was busy at the two-way radio a long time. When

he had finished he sought her out to tell her some news.

'By the way, you're quite a heroine and have come into some money. Thanks to your information those kidnappers have been apprehended at Tobruk and the girl returned to her loving parents apparently unharmed. Your photograph, so I hear, is in all the papers from London to Cairo and W.H.O. has declared itself very proud of you. Sir Wynford Lycett-Houth wants you to spend a weekend at Applewick Castle while he pays you the reward money. What have you to say to all that?'

'I'm very glad the girl's safe,' Sally said sincerely, 'and I'm also glad I'm far enough away from all the hoo-hah. I should hate weekending in Applewick Castle, and as I only did my duty in reporting what I saw I don't expect to be paid for it. Sir Wynford can give the money to charity, if he likes. How about W.H.O. getting it?'

He regarded her with a little more warmth for this outburst and then went off about his own pursuits. She found herself wondering what these would have been if she had really fallen for his charms a couple of nights ago and committed herself. Would Mrs Danely still have been invited to the Villa Inshallah, possibly to give her blessing?

They expected to be at Hidwa for about another week as everything was going so well, but the following morning the medical team received a shock. Yussef was usually the first to wake; it was his job to make the *shai* and take it round. Sally was awakened by his excited chattering through the thin partition which separated her from the men as he shook Darien Marchmont awake. She put on her robe and went to see what was amiss, fearing someone else had been taken ill in the camp.

There simply was no camp, however. Like the Arabs, the Berber tribesmen had folded their tents and silently stolen away. Only a few stakes driven into the sandy soil told where the camel and horse lines had been. There was no litter and even the cooking fires had been carefully exterminated and hidden by sand. All that remained to show there *had* been Berbers there was one fine, fat sheep, which had obviously been left as a gift for the *hakim*.

'This I don't understand,' said Darien Marchmont. 'That wee girl wasn't quite out of the wood.'

Jason explained—they were all up by now—that Madame Doctor had told the chief they could leave after two days.

'I said two weeks,' Sally said sharply. '*Deux semaines.*'

'*Deux jours,*' the other insisted, and looked sulky as Sally opened her mouth to argue. She desisted, however, and looked at Darien Marchmont. 'Very well,' she told him, 'I must take the blame for this, I suppose. When you are not about I find things difficult linguistically. I apparently didn't cope as well as you thought.'

'It's easily done,' he said calmly. 'Bayar was anxious to move on and wanted to believe you said two days. No doubt Fatima will survive. It's the life she's used to when all's said and done, and we pumped quite a lot of penicillin into her. Not to worry. We can check our own stocks and move on ourselves. I only wish they hadn't left this walking lawn-mower behind.' He eyed the sheep gloomily and it baaed in some alarm.

'It's all right, old thing,' he patted its head and examined its wool casually for parasites, wincing away from what he saw.

'You'd better go,' he told Sally. 'There's going to be roast mutton again this evening and I don't propose to roast the creature alive. Yussef!' he called, and Sally fled, wondering what to do with her time now that suddenly there were no patients to attend.

At first, to Sally, Benghazi was the sea, pale green, cool and inviting. She scarcely noticed the dirty little town while she spent hour after hour washing the sand of the desert from her hair, finger and toe-nails and even her eyelashes and brows. If she ever heard the old chestnut of the music halls again, about the 'sand which is there', she would possibly scream, for it was one of those subtle irritants with which one lives for weeks yet does not really register until one is rid of it. To eat food without the crunch of sand in it was suddenly a luxury, and the food at the Vienna Hotel was extremely good and well served. There was hot water in the taps, sprucely kept bathrooms with snowy towels and comfortable beds with disinfectant-fresh sheets. All this was inclined to keep Dr Preston from actual contact with the Benghazi which was outside, however, and there inevitably came the day when she could ignore it no longer.

When she took a walk to the bazaar the day before she was expecting Tom she thought a plague of flies must have descended on the town. She had never seen so many flies in any one place in all her life before. They were black on any edible surface; a vague wave of the hand would temporarily disturb at least two hundred of the creatures from one piece of fish offered for sale, which would descend again in an affronted, buzzing mass the moment the disturbance was removed. Much of the town was still heaps of rubble from the attacks and counter-attacks of the war years, and nobody seemed much concerned with getting it all cleared away and building anew. What building was being done appeared apathetic and there was one half-built skyscraper of concrete which had apparently been abandoned in mid-air. But Benghazi was a friendly place with a happy, smiling populace philosophically waving the flies from their eyes. There appeared to be a high incidence of trachoma and Sally decided to mention this to Darien Marchmont just in case it was any of their business. One could be injected nowadays against the blindness caused by trachoma, but the same apathy which allowed war rubble to lie, making natural depositories for rubbish and breeding grounds for flea-ridden dogs and mangy cats, could well find it too much trouble to inform the populace of this available service.

Having somehow got a sliver of wood into her foot, which was proving extremely painful, Sally took a taxi to the General Hospital for treatment. She could have gone to see Dr Marchmont for this, but she was shy of seeing him off duty and there appeared to be a tacit agreement that for the ten days of their leave they should not meet. She had been firmly instructed to notify him if she should be in any trouble and his telephone number was printed in large black numerals on the fly-leaf of her diary. But Sally was sure that 'trouble' did not include the removal of a splinter from her foot. Her appearance at the Villa Inshallah, with a limp, would appear like an intrusion and an excuse.

The General Hospital was not exactly like any hospital Sally had ever seen. It looked as though it was trying to cope but not quite succeeding, and here again it was the flies which had taken over. These creatures must have developed an airy immunity to D.D.T., for they were everywhere, even walking blithely over the dressings of the surgical patients and swarming over food-trolleys. When it was known she was a doctor, Sally was treated like a V.I.P. and shown round. The wards were gloomy and depressing and food smells, possibly owing to the nature of the fat and spices used, superimposed those of antiseptics.

'It's a big job,' said the Swiss doctor who was escorting Sally. 'We want a new hospital with a large Outpatient Clinic. Why can't there be a Hilton type who would build such hospitals?'

The flies, he explained, died in thousands every day.

'We give them such a strong brew that we nearly kill the patients, too,' he smiled. 'But the trouble is out there'—he cocked his thumb towards the town—'there are always thousands more breeding in open drains and bazaars to take their place. One almost has to accept the fact that there will always be flies in North Africa.'

Sally found that if she gave herself such problems to think about she didn't give so much thought to that terrifying moment of emotional truth between herself and Darien Marchmont. Sometimes she believed it had been so real that all else faded into insignificance beside the experience; at others she had to ask herself if it really had happened. Had she really found herself clasped to Darien Marchmont's breast, breathing hot, exclamatory 'darlings' against his lips so feverishly seeking her own? Such madness she now reproved, and yet such sweetness and promise she could not help regretting. If that was falling in love then she wanted to do it with someone eminently more suitable, who would not laugh at her or deceive her or have other strings to his bow. She supposed that by now Mrs Danely would again have charmed him with her sophisticated presence. He said they had never discussed marriage, but Sally, thinking as a woman, could not see the lovely Serena forsaking her villa in Southern France and flying to Benghazi in September as a simple act of friendship. Whatever Darien intended, Serena already had him tabulated as her most eligible escort.

Tom's plane touched down on the airstrip at ten o'clock next morning. He had flown firstly to Gibraltar, then to Tangier and so 'hopped' on to Benghazi. It was only two days since he had left England and, having a fair complexion, he had not even indulged in the sun of a dubious summer at home.

'It's been a miserable summer back home,' he told Sally as they shook hands after hesitating whether to kiss or not, 'most of the cricket has been washed out.' Tom was a great follower of cricket. It was almost a religion with him and he could never get on with his afternoon's work until he had heard the two o'clock scores. 'You're looking well, Sal,' he added, after taking another rather shy look at her. 'Gosh, isn't it hot!'

Sally suddenly felt sorry for him. He had taken all this trouble to come out and see her, and he hated high temperatures and must be thoroughly uncomfortable with his pink, English complexion and unsuitable clothes. He was even wearing a stiff collar and a tie.

'It must appear hot after all that cool English rain,' she said a little nostalgically, thinking of the garden at home where the big-headed dahlias would be hanging their mop-like heads down to the wet earth and worm-casts would be causing her father to frown over his prized lawn. Actually she hadn't noticed the heat in Benghazi after that sweltering desert journey. Where there was sea one could always imagine oneself cool, for there was the means to becoming so. 'We'll go to the hotel now, Tom, and you can have a shower and change into something cooler.'

Tom appeared for lunch in slacks and an open-necked shirt; his chest was very pink with fuzzy ginger hairs in little curls clustered all over it. He was still perspiring very freely and occasionally patted himself with a large handkerchief.

'Never mind,' Sally smiled, 'you'll become acclimatised very quickly. The secret is not to drink before nightfall if you can help it.'

'I won't be here long enough to become acclimatised, Sal,' he told her, blushing furiously. 'I have to catch the plane back tomorrow.'

She was astounded.

'You mean you came out to Benghazi for only twenty-four hours?' she asked him. 'I thought you had the whole of September for your leave?'

'Yes, I have. But I have a lot to do with it. I have plans, Sal.'

'I'm sure you must have. But *one* day, Tom? Isn't that rather a waste of money?'

'*I* don't think so,' he said gallantly. 'I had to see you, and expense was no object.'

'Well, thank you. Have the curry,' she advised him as the German waiter hovered. 'It's excellent and will cool you down in the long run. Now,' as the waiter went off, 'hadn't you better tell me what you've come about, Tom? There isn't going to be a lot of time.'

'Yes, well,' he havered, 'firstly I'd like to know if you're happy, Sal. Are you doing what you really want to do?'

She had to think about that one.

'You know, Tom, I can't really say. It's been quite an expedition up to now. We were nearly a month dealing with fourteen cases of enteric in the most hopeless conditions, but one isn't happy at such times, merely busy. A lot has happened and much been accomplished. It's a challenging job, full of frustrations, but it's no picnic. I'm glad I came. It will always make a hospital job seem a little tame by comparison.'

'What's this Marchmont like?'

Sally was glad she was tanned. She hoped her rising colour didn't show at the mention of that name.

'He's very clever and—and nice,' she said lamely.

'I know of him,' Tom said surprisingly. 'He's one of the Ulster Marchmonts from Dhu-derry. His father doctored in India. Pots of money. His grandfather was quite a philanthropist and started a medical foundation in Northern Ireland. I suppose that's where the family got its inspiration from. There's an elder brother who's a Professor of Surgery in some university. This one—Darien, isn't it?—is noted for doing rotten jobs in awful places. He was in refugee camps before he joined World Health. I suppose it's one way of making up to mankind for being so well off.'

Sally lapped up all this information like a sponge and then said defensively, 'It's not a disease being well off, is it, Tom?'

'No, I suppose not,' he sighed. 'If so we would all want to catch it. At least, I would.'

'Well, perhaps you'll tell me why you flung about a hundred hard-earned pounds away in coming to see me in the middle of my job? I expect to be home by Christmas and we could have met then.'

'That would have been too late, Sal. You see I—wanted you to be the first to know that I'm thinking of getting married.'

Her eyes widened in surprise and then a slow smile spread over her countenance.

'No!' she exclaimed. 'Well done!'

He looked relieved at her reaction.

'So you don't mind?' he asked.

'Now why should I mind? You're a free agent, Tom. I thought we both made that clear when we parted in London that day. You don't mean to say that you thought I ought to be told in person in case I committed suicide? Whatever we meant to one another, Tom, it simply wasn't enough. I'm really glad you appear to have found someone more suitable. Who is she?'

'Well, her name's Avril and she came to work in the lab just after you left England. I wanted to tell you because I think these things are awful if you read about them in the papers. I know I would have minded reading about you like that, if I hadn't got Avril, that is. Now I hope you'll find somebody, Sal. I want you to be happy, too.'

'Well, thank you, Tom. I expect one day I'll find this Mr Right they talk about.'

'Darien Marchmont's a good prospect,' Tom said mischievously. 'Why can't you fall in love with him?'

'I can see falling in love has made you skittish, Tom Rydale,' she took refuge in teasing, 'but I must keep that suggestion in mind for the future. I may be a gold-digger at heart and perhaps you were lucky to escape in time. When's the wedding?'

'Ah, yes. I can now tell Avril it's O.K. for next week and then we can get our honeymoon in during my leave.'

'You don't mean to say poor Avril has been kept in suspense pending my approval? Oh, Tom! When will you make a bold decision without shilly-shallying? I despair of you. You might lose the girl unless you send her a cable immediately, and don't forget to tell her you love her. After wasting a hundred pounds on this trip you can't skimp on three extra words to your future wife. Go and do it now. Such things have a very slow start in places like this.'

Tom went off quite happily, his shirt soaked between his shoulder-blades.

'How could I ever have thought romantically of Tom!' Sally marvelled as she scraped up what remained of the curry on her plate. 'I wonder if he feels, with Avril, what I felt with Darien? Has he got it in him? I don't think so, somehow. I can't imagine Darien asking anybody's permission to do something his heart was firmly set on. I can't believe that everything is over between us, if he really meant it to start. He simply wouldn't be discouraged so easily.'

The thought made her thrill unaccountably, but she brought sanity back by reminding herself that he wasn't good for her. He made her forget herself, and that wouldn't do at all. One ought always to be in command of oneself, the captain of one's soul.

Tom returned to the table so absurdly delighted with his future prospects that Sally was touched for him.

'We won't go sightseeing,' she told him, 'because I want to hear all about Avril and I'm sure you'll want to talk about her. Let's spend the afternoon on the beach, swimming and lazing. Would you like that?'

'It sounds delightful,' he enthused. 'I'll just go and get my trunks.'

Sally was bowing her lips with the flame-coloured lipstick which complemented her tan when the pain suddenly struck and made her scalp tingle.

'Aah!' She relaxed from its clutches in some relief as the spasm passed and mentally sought the origin of the trouble.

'Definitely not my appendix; that came out when I was sixteen. Anyway, it was rather higher. Probably something I ate.'

The second gripe left her in no doubt that her stomach was the seat of the disorder. She unchained herself from the pain and was violently sick for a few minutes, immediately feeling greatly relieved.

'Oh, thank heaven! I don't want to spoil Tom's one

and only day with a bilious attack. That may have been it. I'll take a dose of Milk of Magnesia and hope for the best.'

The trouble kept at bay while they took a taxi to the more salubrious part of the beach where the sand was sifted as fine as dust and hot to the feet.

'Gosh!' laughed Tom. 'One can get blisters in a place like this in awkward spots.'

Sally tried to think she was enjoying her swim, but the pain struck again so that she blanched perceptibly and looked faintly green under her tan.

'What's up?' Tom asked, noting this.

'I don't think the curry agreed with me, or it may have been a piece of melon I had this morning. Have you noticed the flies here? I'll be all right.'

When the colour returned she really did look normal, but it disappeared for whole minutes at a time while knives apparently carved up her vitals.

'Look here, Sal, dry yourself and get dressed. We must go back to the hotel. Have you got something you can take for it?'

'A couple of doctors,' she joked heavily, 'we should be able to manage. Just put me to bed, Tom, and leave me to get on with it.'

He wasn't going to do anything of the kind, however. He was prepared to do a lot more.

'If you're no better tomorrow, Sal, I'm not going to leave you. No use arguing,' he said as he at last tucked her into bed with the help of the hotel manageress. 'I'm not familiar with the local bugs, and although it seems to be a bout of gastro-enteritis I would be happier if you had a wash-out, my girl. I'm going to contact the hospital and ask if they can deal with you.'

' 'Ospital?' the manageress echoed sharply. 'No. Not for Madame. 'Ospital too crowded and not enough staff. Just a minute. I use telephone.'

'I suppose she knows what she's doing,' Tom said uneasily as he held the bowl for the patient yet once again and examined the skimpy contents with pathological interest. He desperately wanted his own laboratory with its neat glass jars lining the walls and well-scrubbed marble working tops. Here he felt inadequate. He was no Marchmont to be able to work in refugee camps and Arab tents.

That was the answer. He must get in touch with Marchmont. The fellow couldn't be far away.

Tom ran downstairs to seek out the manageress and ask if she knew where Dr Marchmont could be contacted.

'Dr Marchmont, 'e is coming,' the woman said promptly. 'I telephone.'

'Thank you. Thank you very much.'

'It is nothing. Dr Marchmont ask that I keep an eye on Madame. He would not want her to go to our 'ospital. 'Ospitals are fine, but many lack ze—ze—facilities of European 'ospitals. You know, overcrowding, flies, domestic workers who do not wash 'ands? Zat is not for such a pretty little lady, I sink?'

Tom trailed back upstairs where Sally was lying in a pool of sweat, looking waxen and not quite of this world. Her abdominal muscles convulsed as he watched and he held the bowl to her lips, but nothing came. She flopped back wearily against the pillows with a small strangled cry.

'Oh, Tom!'

Dr Tom Rydale had never been so glad to see another member of his profession as when Darien Marchmont, thunder-browed in his anxiety, strode through the door and took charge.

CHAPTER ELEVEN

DARIEN MARCHMONT had never found himself less disposed to enjoy himself than when he found himself in the familiar surroundings of the Villa Inshallah with time on his hands. It was a handsome villa overlooking about an acre of beach, pebble-strewn rather than sandy. It was his beach, but he did not seal it off from those less fortunate. Even the villa was more often occupied than not by weary medicos and their families. It was usually advertised in the *British Medical Journal* and the proceeds went to medical charities. A sturdy Northern Irish housekeeper kept the place spick and span and had trained her staff in British culinary arts in addition to their own native skills so that the villa's menus were often a creation of the best of both worlds.

The stony beach was no drawback, for the villa had its own swimming-pool and a paved surround which was unique in that many of the ornamental tiles were of Greek origin, excavated when the foundations of the house had been dug, and handed back to Doctor Marchmont after examination by the experts.

It always gave Darien a thrill to step out of his pool and pause on a tile which may have accommodated a Greek explorer after *his* bath more than two thousand years ago. He always hoped that it was a student of Hippocrates who had lived here, maybe doctoring the troops who had been the originators of Cyrenaica.

Somehow his arrival at Villa Inshallah on this occasion had been a disappointment to himself if not to his staff, who were always delighted to see him. There were no other visitors in occupation at the moment, although this would not have inconvenienced him in the slightest as his own apartments were self-contained from the main building. Here he kept spare clothes and books and the tools of his occupation, reference books, a microscope and various instruments. Serena had cabled that Jeremy had mumps and so her visit would be delayed until she could get someone to take the child over and release her. He felt fairly irritated that she should consider leaving her small son at such a time. The child was inclined to delicacy—he had bouts of bronchial asthma—and as these occurred with greater frequency at times when his mother was absent, Darien was inclined to link the two facts and believe that a mother's place was with her child.

'Now look here,' Serena had told him sharply in Tangier a few months ago, 'Jerry just has to learn to do without me sooner or later. I'd have a five-year-old baby if you had your way, Darien. He deliberately precipitates these attacks to get attention, you know. I have only to come into his room and they miraculously get better. You really don't know the first thing about children, do you? What Jerry really needs is a father. He wants a firm hand. I love my boy, but I'm not going to sacrifice myself for him. I, too, am young—'

Darien could picture the dark, mysterious pools of her eyes as she spoke. She was a very lovely woman; it had been hell when she had announced she was marrying George Danely. But behind the mask of mystery was a basic competence to cope with any eventuality, even the sudden death of her husband. With time's passing Darien Marchmont realised that Serena didn't need any man save as a necessary adjunct to her feminine vanity. She was lovelier, if possible, in maturity and enjoyed quite a gay life. About twice a year she contrived to spend some time with Darien, whom she was aware had once adored her. He enjoyed their meetings, for she could be extremely charming and gracious and she was always pleasing to the sight.

He had wondered, after she had flown from the airport at Tangier, if they should discuss marriage some time. He was now thirty-five and normally interested in the opposite sex. He had always believed in, and waited hopefully for, an emotional experience of such magnitude that it would be instantly recognisable and eminently satisfying. Lately he had decided this cataclysm was never going to happen, and as his instincts were not those of a confirmed bachelor he had practically decided to put the ball in Serena's court and ask her if she thought they might make a go of a union.

Some spanner had fallen into the works of these plans just lately, however. The hoped-for cataclysm had almost happened, right out of the blue, or rather the black and moon-washed gold of a desert night. He had suddenly found himself struggling with the dragons of his self-control with a creature like a fairy unaccountably in his arms.

How this eventuality had actually occurred he still didn't quite know. His young colleague amused and intrigued him; often she infuriated him; he couldn't imagine such a scrap of sheer femininity ever surviving the rigours of medical school, let alone qualifying to trudge alongside him so manfully in the wilderness. He felt like an indulgent uncle with her much of the time. She had been so shy after that incident in the swimming-pool in Tangier, and shyness was something he did not associate with modern young women, though it was nevertheless a quality he appreciated in the female on account of its appeal rather than its rarity.

When he had forced her to play that part of the sweetheart for El Bashir's lecherous-eyed benefit, he had simply been playing, though he had enjoyed holding her, rebellious and helpless, in his power. It was a role he could have maintained for much longer than had been permissible, without becoming bored by the game.

After that, at Hidwa, he had been forced to admire that scrap of a creature as she waded in up to her neck to help him tackle the epidemic, loathsome as this could be without proper facilities. He could still see her, wringing with sweat, her ridiculous little 'chukka' boots grey with dust, helping to hump buckets of infection-ridden faeces to the lime-pit dug to receive it. She had never cried for quarter or attempted to bypass an unpleasant job. He had already determined to award her the accolade of honourable mention in his reports. No man could have done better, perhaps not as much, for Dr Preston, conscious that her sex was always questioned in a field which had been the prerogative of men for so long, was inclined to exceed her expected capacity in order to make sure that this was enough.

When she complained of a headache on the night of the chief-making, he had felt tender towards her. The end of labour was in sight and the poor lassie was at last wilting a little. She must be bored, too, and missing all that she had left behind her in gay London. They would walk and chat for a while; he would make an effort to befriend her.

But what had actually happened did not appear to

have required any effort but a mutual, somewhat irrational sympathy. Darien had kissed many women, had extracted enjoyment from the experience, but he had never before felt the urge to hurl himself into a bottomless pit of emotional revelation. It was not merely that kissing Sara on the lips was profoundly stirring; it was some answering response from her to him which had caused a sudden eruption and narrowed the world down to the single fact that together they became one perfect human entity. Of course one sprang back in time to reason, one didn't fall into the pit, but it had been there and could never be forgotten. Obviously this Dr Preston was a force to be reckoned with. In a way he had been glad she had told him to stop the nonsense—it gave him time to think—but thinking was no conclusion in itself. He wanted to go on with her, work upwards from the plane of that physical collision which he knew to be only one interesting facet of a perfect relationship.

She didn't seem to be willing to continue, however, and there was every possibility that she was already committed. As a gentleman he could only accept what she was prepared to offer. He couldn't take her by brute force. When he had seen the Mantelons off and returned to camp to find her apparently prepared to forgive and forget, offering the hand of friendship but nothing more close than that, then he had, like a beggar, accepted the crumbs of a relationship. He had a new respect for her; as a lamp must respect the match which lights it; but as twin luminaries they were for the moment burnt out and needed time to recuperate from many things.

He had been genuinely hurt by Sara's refusal of hospitality in Benghazi. He had looked forward to showing her the villa, the old story-ridden tiles, the pale azure of the pool and Miss McNeill's gastronomic furbishings as a background to long hours of restful conversation which would enable them to know one another so much better. Actually they knew so little about each other apart from the fact that together they had the potential of a generating force worthy of the respect of Niagara Falls, but when one didn't know whether the other preferred grand opera to *My Fair Lady*, or Ibsen to Coward, then there was plenty of room for the acquaintance to develop.

Sara had been kind but very firm in her preference for accommodation in a hotel rather than Inshallah, however, and when it was known she had a man visitor in the offing, this was understandable. It was a kind of blind retaliation which made Darien send for Serena, but in reality he dreaded the meeting. Serena had always been there, she had been, to him, almost an ideal of womanhood, and now she was suddenly deposed in his sight. Even the remembrance of her seemed less than life-size, suddenly. He now brooded that she had glaring faults in her character, that she became outraged over trivialities such as being kept waiting a few minutes and also found her small, clinging son a nuisance. Children, to Serena, were like parcels, nice to have so long as they could be dumped on somebody else.

Now, seeing Serena clearly, he had to take a fresh look at himself. Why was he suddenly dissatisfied, nervous, unsure of the way ahead? It must be obvious to any half-baked lady novelist that he was evincing all the signs of falling in love for the first time rather late in his career and that he didn't know how to let his heart state his case. He had already driven the lady into some other fellow's arms. She hadn't been near the villa and could apparently get on very well without him.

For days Darien Marchmont was moody, broody, vaguely uneasy and at a loss. When the manageress of the Vienna Hotel telephoned that his colleague was ill his first reaction was relief that he was, apparently, necessary for her if only in his professional capacity. Only secondarily was he smitten by a blind panic which was as unreasoning as a nightmare as it ravaged his mind with improbabilities.

Could she have caught enteric? Maybe her jabs had not wholly immunised her and the strain of the past few weeks had laid her wide open to attack. He leapt into his hired car and hurtled along the wide road between other white villas like his own. An itinerant Arab, driving two goats, appeared from the beach and casually crossed the road, causing him to brake hard. The Arab muttered that the son-of-a-dog white man was in too much of a hurry, and was surprised when his own tongue was lashed back at him to the effect that it was better to be the son of a dog and live than to be the son of an ass and throw one's life away. The Arab now smiled toothily, full of respect, and Darien drove on through the meaner streets of Benghazi, past the bazaars and the bomb sites and so to the Vienna with its courtyard of cosseted pot plants and its faded blinds.

In the bedroom he saw Sara first of all and then her companion.

'How d'you do, sir,' this person said almost deferentially, holding out a pink hand, 'I'm Rydale.'

'I'm Marchmont.'

'Yes, I know. Sally's a bit under the weather.'

'How much under the weather?'

'I'm not sure. I didn't know whether she'd care for me examining her.' Tom laughed foolishly. 'I kept a specimen for you to see.'

Darien said, 'Do you want me to look at her, Dr Rydale?'

Tom looked surprised at being asked. It was so long since he had been personally associated with patients that sometimes he forgot specimens came from people.

'Please do,' he said promptly.

Sally said with some peevishness from the bed, 'When you two have finished being ethical I would like the bowl, please.'

Darien obliged with a smile. She had been very much herself for a moment there. Obviously there was nothing terribly amiss. Her brow was damp with perspiration for one thing, so there was no fever. He made his examination efficiently and without embarrassment. He caught the gleam of a brown eye as his probing fingers found and investigated a tender spot.

'No rigidity anywhere and no enlargement,' he told her kindly. 'You know the drill for gastro-enteritis, the only difference here being that all water must be boiled.'

She said, drawing the sheet up, 'Thank you, sir, I'm sorry to break in on your leave.'

'I've been expecting you—both,' he said, looking up at Tom.

'May I have a word with you?' asked that worthy, indicating that they converse outside.

'Actually I was flying out tomorrow,' Tom confided when they were alone. 'Is there any need for me to stay on? I mean, I don't want to leave poor old Sal ill in a hotel.'

'And do you have to go? I thought you would have wanted to——'

'Well, I do, actually,' Tom said, ignoring the second statement. 'I'm getting married next week.'

147

Hope stirred like a hatching bird in Darien's breast. He still couldn't quite believe in such a stroke of luck.

'I'm afraid I was thinking that you and Dr Preston were . . .'

Tom laughed again and blushed his big, pink blush. 'Yes—well, we used to be. But Sal had more sense than to put up with me. She's a go-ahead sort of girl and I'm a stick-in-the-mud chap.'

'I'm sure not,' Darien said politely.

'So what arrangements can we make for her?' Tom persisted. 'I don't suppose she's bad enough for hospital?'

'No. Don't worry, my dear chap, I'll take her back with me. That way I'll be able to supervise her diet and so forth.' Darien sounded very pleased with this arrangement even to his own ears. He had to batten down his obvious pleasure while he informed the patient of his decision.

'I don't want to be a nuisance,' Sally protested weakly. 'I'll do very well here by myself.'

'There's no question of your staying here,' he told her firmly. 'In fact I'm taking you with me now. There's no need to fuss. All you need is a robe to put round you. Your clothes can be collected later. You'll feel terrible if you try to stand. Just relax and leave everything to me, as your doctor, will you?'

Sally had to give in, she felt so terrible and dizzy with nausea whenever she lifted her head. She was glad of strong arms which lifted her gently and carried her down the stairs as though she was a mere doll. Tom said goodbye and kissed her on the cheek. It had been short but very sweet, he told her, and then she was glad to curl up in the back of a car and suffer her pain without fear because of that strong, upright figure at the wheel which would inspire anybody with confidence. She felt temporarily a little better as the car turned in at a wide drive under pink oleanders which sweetened the air headily.

'What does "Inshallah" mean, sir?' she asked.

'It means God's Will, Sara. You must remember that, it's a good thing to submit to.'

The attack did not incapacitate her for long and Sally wondered at the attentions to which she was submitted for far longer than she considered necessary. Darien Marchmont appeared to enjoy having her for a patient; his visits to her room were protracted and Miss McNeill conjured up all manner of dainties to encourage an appetite which was very quickly back to normal.

'I really *could* get up,' she insisted at the end of her second day in bed, though she had luxuriated in the cosseting she had received at the hands of the doctor and his staff alike. 'I feel a fraud lying here and doing nothing.'

'Take it easy,' he warned her. 'These things always take some getting over. It's so easy to have another attack on top of the first. Tomorrow you can perhaps get up and try a swim in the pool and then sit in a lounging chair out of the sun. You're doing fine, so leave the rest to me.'

CHAPTER TWELVE

She suspected that out of many fine rooms she must have been given the best in the house. The walls were coolly white, with intricately carved Spanish wrought-iron wall-lights at regular intervals. There was a white Chinese carpet on a red-tesselated floor and the furniture was Mediterranean antique apart from the bed, which was large and white with a satin-studded head-board and quilted bedspread, knotted with tiny pink rosebuds. The triple-windows were part of a corner tower and one could walk out on to an encircling balcony awninged with a red and white blind, deeply fringed. The view was breathtaking—a white-pebbled beach and blue rollers riding in with the swish of expensive silk, lace-edged. The sound of the sea was never angry, always narcotic. The heat was kept at bay by an insulating plant and one had only to step out on to the balcony to realise that it really was there, searing and softened only by the breath of the hot wind. It was a place one couldn't wish to leave in a hurry, especially when one's doctor had practically commanded one to stay.

Sally therefore forbore to argue as she spent her next day in and out of the pool and in a large, comfortable, cane-hooded lounging chair. The luncheon chicken was in aspic and served with salad. They took it out of doors under a shady eucalyptus tree.

'The disinfectant aroma keeps pests away,' Darien explained. 'Could you eat more?'

Sally could and did.

'I'm perfectly all right again,' she had to admit. 'I think I'd better go back to the hotel. I've imposed upon your hospitality long enough.'

'Imposed—? My dear young lady, there's plenty of room here. You're most welcome to——'

'I shall feel terrible unless you let me go back,' she felt bound to demur. 'We have to see each other at work, but this is leave and you have a right to your privacy. I am grateful, but——'

'There's no room in the hotel now,' he said quickly. 'I had your things brought here and told Madame to let your apartment. I rather thought I would like to keep an eye on you.'

She stared at him.

'I don't know what to say. I don't want to intrude. You have your own friends, and——'

'I would like to include you in that category at least,' he said, and his eyes fell momentarily in some embarrassment. 'I wonder if you can ever forget that I upset you so deeply, Sara? It troubles me that you're apparently nervous of being in my company. I don't mean to force it on you against your will. You can enjoy the villa, its amenities, without having to endure me, you know. Just say the word and I'll keep clear of you. I can be entirely self-contained in my own apartments.'

She had blushed a deep, rich red, but her voice was steady as she replied.

'I harbour no resentment or sense of grievance against you for what happened in the past, Darien. I was a most willing accessory, and that must be stated categorically. I don't think we either of us gave much thought to what happened at the time; we allowed our emotions to carry us along—or perhaps I speak for myself—and that sort of headlong career must be short-lived for everyone's sake. I'm only nervous in your company because I feel like a trespasser. If I may be absolutely frank, having been in your arms I feel I know you on that plane only, which is rather disconcerting. A stranger keeps popping up that I don't know. I think we plunged into our relationship at the wrong end first, if you understand.'

'That can always be remedied,' he said, looking happier. 'I think I would rather like to know you, too.'

'But we must forget that other time. After all, we had been together, thrust on each other, for a long time. I think a safety valve blew for both of us. I don't expect anything of you because of what happened.'

'If those are your terms,' he said sincerely, 'I accept them. We can be friends and—well, let what will develop.' She blushed again with her hand in his sealing the pact of friendship and he lifted her chin to say, 'I'm intrigued when you do that. It's not at all just— friendly, and I for one can't wait for the kissing to start again. But I'm a patient man. I can bide my time while you're finding out if knowing me is to love me.'

She suddenly laughed uninhibitedly, feeling life to be full of wonderful possibilities and laid out like an intricately patterned carpet for her to tread on.

'And you *will* stay?' he asked, gazing intently into her eyes.

'I'll stay, and thank you for asking me,' she told him. 'How much longer is there before we go back to work?'

'Three days and then I'll leave you here, lotus-eating, while I push on to Alexandria to see what the Area Office has made of our Outward Bound trip and to get instructions for the next leg. But we'll live one day at a time and there's still half of this one. How would you like a sail? Can you crew for me if I tell you what to do?'

'I would love to try. The women I've seen in boats, hanging out over the water, always look like Amazons to me. Am I big enough to be of any use?'

'You're very nicely displaced for my purpose,' he opined, surveying her appreciatively. 'When the boom comes across you're less likely to get in the way. A decapitated Amazon is not a pretty sight.'

It was a very pleasant and most exciting afternoon's sport. The small, trim yacht was top-heavy with sail and made tremendous speed when they successfully caught the off-shore breezes. Darien was tousled and happy while Sally, looking like some creature from the deep as she leant out over the water acting as human ballast, soaked in spray and not caring one iota, shrieked her delight at intervals.

'You're soaked to the skin,' Darien told her as they transferred to a dinghy and a hired boy took the yacht back to berth in the deeper waters of the harbour. 'Better have a bath and change when we get home.'

She liked the sound of that 'home'. It sounded cosy and rather intimate.

'I don't know when I had a more attractive crew,' he told her. 'I would like to say well done in my own way.'

'Which is——?' she asked, pausing on the shingle and regarding him, strangely at one with this man and knowing exactly what was coming. When his lips descended there was no shocked surprise on her part. She simply did her part in the kissing and stood back, her brown eyes warmly upon his. The control behind that salute intrigued her. This was no runaway romance at this point. They both knew they had taken another first step towards something wonderful which promised, only this time their heads were keeping pace with their hearts.

Taking her hand in his, he started to run over the shingle towards the house as though his exuberance could scarcely be controlled.

'I'm hungry!' he shouted. 'I hope Miss McNeill is preparing something wonderful for dinner. We'll go out to a night club, shall we? I shall keep you out until dawn. There's all day for the arms of Morpheus, but *my* arms——' he stopped their headlong career and his words dried in his throat. Stepping out daintily across the shingle, in high heels, a set smile on her beautiful face and hauling a small, pale child by the hand, was the dark woman Sally had last seen in the foyer of El Minzah.

'Serena!' Darien said, almost disbelievingly. 'I'd given you up.'

Sally found her hand released and she was suddenly conscious of the sight she must look beside this coutured perfection with her hair plastered to her head and her blouse and shorts sticking to her like a second skin.

Darien made the introductions, 'Serena Danely; *Dr* Preston,' and then swung the little boy into the air with a great deal of squealing and to-do.

'It's always like this when they meet,' Mrs Danely said coolly and apologetically. 'Nobody else gets a look in. Darien dotes on Jerry. He *should* have been his father.'

Sally had the impression that the day had grown very much cooler, but realised her own damp state might account for this.

'I really must get out of these things and have a bath, Mrs Danely,' she said when they reached the house. 'Will you excuse me?'

'Certainly, Dr Preston,' the other said with a slight inclination of her lovely head. 'You must want to look dainty and feminine again. I would never allow Darien to take me in his wretched yacht, but I can see you're an easier touch than I am.' Sally did not know whether to feel annoyed at this or not, but allowed it to pass. 'There's one thing, Dr Preston,' the other continued, 'I've had your things moved into another room. I knew you wouldn't mind. I usually have that suite when I visit Inshallah because it has a connecting room where Jerry likes to sleep. Miss McNeill will tell you where to go.'

Sally tried hard to believe that the day had not been ruined. She and Darien had had the best part of it together and things had been said and done which could not lightly be forgotten. But her lips were set with annoyance as the housekeeper apologetically showed her to her new room, one overlooking the courtyard at the side of the house.

'I'm that sorry you've had to shift, Doctor, but Mrs Danely has been coming to the villa for a number of years and always has the tower room. She sort of expects it nowadays.'

'I don't mind moving at all,' Sally insisted, privately minding more and more as she thought about it. 'I shall be very comfortable here.'

She didn't see Darien again until dinner, though she could hear him playing with the little boy. Presiding over the dinner-table was Mrs Danely. For a few minutes the two women were alone.

'Darien is putting Jerry to bed,' Serena explained. 'He does it so well and the boy heeds him so much better than he does me. I never have any trouble with Jerry once he knows Darien is on hand. Of course he is rather trying. He has asthmatic attacks, you know. I feel I can't leave him without someone experienced in charge. A baby-sitter simply isn't enough unless she happens to be a doctor or nurse. I say, I've just thought. You're a doctor and you're right here on the spot. Would you mind taking over while Darien and I go out on the town?'

Sally felt temporarily stunned. The cheek of the woman!

'Of course if you would rather not——?' Serena said reproachfully, surveying the dinner-table and re-arranging the crystal glasses with musical tinkles.

'I shall be happy to help out,' Sally found herself saying, rather ashamed of her hesitation, 'if you think I'll prove adequate. You must tell me what to do for the child if he wakes up with an attack.'

'Sweet of you,' Serena flashed, as Darien came into the room apologising for his lateness. 'That's all right, darling,' she tossed at him with a brilliant smile. 'We haven't missed you one bit. We know you men really prefer one another's company to ours, don't we, Dr Preston? By the way, Darien, this charming assistant of yours has just volunteered to stay and keep an eye on your godson while we go out this evening. Isn't that civil of her?'

Darien glanced questioningly at Sally, who coloured up to her eyebrows.

'Very civil,' he agreed drily. 'I rather thought she had other plans.'

'Well, they can't have been terribly important, darling, and I'll make it up to her in some way. It will be just like old times, you and I *tête-à-tête*. Are you engaged or anything, Dr Preston?'

'Not engaged or anything,' Sally smiled somewhat wryly.

'Not even a little bit of "anything"?' Darien smiled

encouragingly, daring her to meet his eyes. 'I rather thought you were entertaining hopes of a future alliance.'

'Hopes are one thing, sir,' she told him, 'but plans are quite another.'

'So you see, darling?' Serena blandly enquired. 'Don't pry into the poor girl's private business. He's a devil for his fun,' she explained to Sally as they took their places at table. 'Beware of his Irish sense of humour. I would never take him seriously on any subject excepting his unquestionable devotion to my small son. You must never believe a single thing he says. It's all part of a natural gift of the blarney.'

'I never even saw Blarney Castle,' snorted Darien. 'I'm an Ulsterman by heredity though I was born in India, and my sense of humour at the moment is null and void.'

'Oh, poor darling!' Serena sympathised, wrinkling her attractive nose. 'You *have* been missing me! I couldn't help Jerry getting mumps, you know, and I came as soon as I could, even though I had to drag the little devil with me once he knew where I was going.' She turned confidingly to Sally. 'Motherhood can be quite a strain on a widow, Dr Preston. Any child needs a man in his life, especially a boy. I do try to be firm, but——'

'You're joking,' Darien said with heavy sarcasm. 'Neither you nor the lad has the least inkling as to the meaning of discipline, and you know it.'

'Don't be a bear, darling. You can always show us. You know how you love being superior and tough and we both adore it. I want to discuss schools with you when you have a moment. It must be faced that your godson has to be fittingly educated.' Once again she turned on a smile for Sally's benefit. 'I must apologise most humbly, Dr Preston. You're obviously thinking we've forgotten you're here. As such old, tried friends Darien and I must be excused for hogging the conversation on this first evening of our reunion.'

'I quite understand that you must have a great deal to discuss,' Sally said quietly.

'But we needn't discuss it over the dinner table,' Darien cut in brightly, 'because we're going out together, aren't we, Serena? What will you do, Dr Sara, this evening?'

'I'll most probably read, sir.' She did not raise her eyes as she said this.

'Good! I'll lend you my Rubá'iyát, which you never got around to borrowing as yet. One can never read too much of old Khayyam. The thirty-second and the fifty-sixth stanzas stick in my mind at the moment as being applicable to that discussion we had recently. See what you think.'

Serena said, 'Oh, how amusing! You work together and discuss obsolete poets in your spare time. Thank goodness you don't bore me with such stuff, Darien.'

He smiled, everyone was smiling, yet nobody was in the least lighthearted or happy. Serena was thinking, 'I should have got here earlier. There's something here which must quickly be snuffed out. Darien has never looked at another woman all these years and yet I saw them kissing openly down on the beach for anybody to see. I know it didn't mean anything, or rather I hope it didn't, because I haven't decided I don't want Darien for myself yet. I would have encouraged him years ago if it wasn't for this bee he's got in his bonnet about doing awful jobs in awful places. He's quite the most attractive man I know, and Jerry eats out of his hand. I have to think of myself. This woman is too young to be safe. These nonentities are always on the lookout with a view to improving their status, and Darien would improve anybody's status, even mine. I'm glad he's moving off soon and leaving his assistant to my care. I can't wait to tell her where she gets off, though I must do it skilfully, of course.'

Sally was thinking, 'What an awful end to a most wonderful day! Now that she's here I feel very much the odd one out in a party of three. Did Darien mean what he said, or was it because I was the only one available? I wouldn't have dreamed of doubting him if it wasn't for Mrs Danely and all her proprietorial "darlings". To hear her one would think they were only waiting for the third reading of the banns before going to the altar. And Darien's behaving very peculiarly towards me and I can't make him out at all. Eden must have been like this after the serpent got in. Everybody's talking in riddles. I wish this wretched meal was over. I haven't enjoyed a thing.'

Darien Marchmont, too, felt more like one of the three witches in Macbeth, huddled over a cauldron of boiling, poisonous substance, than the handsome host with two attractive young women at his table. These two should have complemented each other, he pondered darkly, but in fact one of them was like a snuffed-out candle and the other was blazing forth like a beacon, bright enough for the two of them. But he did not like Serena in this mood; he felt she was trapping him in a goo of friendship as though he was a fly caught in a spider's web. He preferred her standing him off, being cool and serene and beautiful, also unobtainable. That she appeared to be offering herself at sale price shocked him not a little; she was constantly telling Sara how close they were and how the boy needed him and what ages she had come to his beck to queen it in his house. He was angry with Sara for so easily breaking their date for the evening, too. Serena could have looked after her own kid or they could have gone out in a threesome. If young Jerry wakened up after the hour's horseplay they had enjoyed together then he was a Dutchman. He didn't believe Serena's assertion that he woke up every night with asthma, and in any case he was old enough to take his pill if he needed it. Asthmatics and diabetics simply had to learn to cope with their disabilities, and the sooner the better. Still, it had been a rotten dinner-party and he was glad when the ladies decided to leave him to his brandy and disappeared together.

'I'll be ready in an hour, darling,' Serena called loudly and unnecessarily.

He had to admit that in maturity she was even more lovely than when he had first known her, but her beauty struck him now as being as cold and calculated as something hanging in the Louvre. It had only one expression which was strictly beautiful; anger must not be allowed to ravage it or ecstasy to colour. It was a flat, matt statement. Serena somehow seemed to have given up living. Or was it that the lively little Dr Preston made this appear to be so by the supposed odium of comparison?

Nobody could call Sara Preston static. She was both quick to anger and eager for experience. He never quite knew what next to expect of her quicksilver mind and her powers of endurance had always amazed him. She was unpredictable and, was he ever to possess her, he would never be absolutely sure what to expect from her. Life would be one long, glorious uncertainty with such a wife, her countenance at one moment appealing with the candour of a child and at another maternal and ageless.

Today he had found himself thrilling again to the

new discovery of her, holding himself in check so as not to scare her into cutting and running yet once again. But she hadn't even tried to run. Her eyes had looked into his and made a promise, and only Serena's untimely interruption had stopped him from turning the intangibility of a glance into the reality of words.

Why had she been so dumbstruck during dinner, then? Why didn't she, by her attitude, encourage him to tell Serena they never intended stopping at being 'old friends' themselves? He couldn't say it alone, not without her permission, but he knew it was dangerous to allow Serena to go on thinking he would always be available.

He suddenly hated brandy and wanted only another, blither spirit. He had to see her, without Serena knowing. Picking up a morocco-bound copy of the Rubá'iyát, he went along to the Tower room.

Serena, in a negligée, wrapped herself around him and offered her red lips.

'Darling! Couldn't you wait to be alone with me? I've missed you, too. Kiss me! Kiss me!' The dark eyes slowly became watchful and glanced up. 'What's the matter, then? Is it the way I'm dressed? Oh, darling, don't be an old prude. After all, if we're going to be married . . .'

Darien sighed patiently and put her away from him.

'What is all this, Serena? I wasn't aware it was a Leap Year and ladies' privilege. You turned me down as a marital proposition at one time, and I assure you I haven't changed from the man I was then.'

'Maybe I have, darling,' she crooned after a moment's thought. 'You're just what the doctor ordered for me nowadays. I want to make you happy and I know you adore Jerry.'

'I *like* young Jerry. What an extravagant creature

you've become with words, Serena. You know we would fight like cat and dog, if we married, you've always said so, and I entirely agree. Some relationships thrive for never being allowed to become intimate. Ours is one of them. Don't tell me you're short of attractive escorts all at once?' he asked in lighter vein.

'No,' she answered him dubiously, 'but Jerry would be happy with you. Not everyone has patience with a delicate child.'

He put his hands on her shoulders very firmly and looked down at her. 'When you marry again, Serena,' he told her, 'do it for love and not because of Jerry. Anybody who really cares about you will accept your child exactly as he is, and don't go around calling him delicate. I've seen kiddies like him at five years old turn into rough-and-ready young hooligans by the time they were ten. He'll grow out of this complaint if only you would stop reminding him of it. Do believe that, my dear. Now I must go and get ready.'

'Why *did* you come to my room, Darien?' she asked as he reached the door.

'For this little chat, of course,' he said quickly, wondering at her curiosity.

'Oh. I thought you might have expected to find your colleague here, perhaps.'

He turned to regard her speculatively.

'Have you everything you need, Serena?' He didn't intend to make her a gift of a catch if she was merely fishing.

'Everything, I think,' she told him demurely, and narrowed her dark eyes as he went out leaving his copy of the Rubá'iyát behind him on the nearby chair. She had heard that exchange between the doctor colleagues at the dinner-table, had suspected that the verses he had mentioned were meant to be of significance to them and no one else. Being far more astute than she ever allowed Darien to believe her, she had memorised the numbers of the stanzas for future reference if necessary. After Darien's rebuff she now felt the necessity of this move and scrabbled through the pages of the slim volume, fearing Darien's imminent return when he should discover his remissness.

'Stupid old bore!' was her opinion of the Persian poet as she had some difficulty deciphering the roman numerals of the stanza headings. When she did find number thirty-two she felt no happer for reading it. She didn't like its tone one little bit.

> *'There was a door to which I found no key:*
> *There was a veil past which I could not see;*
> *Some little talk awhile of Me and Thee*
> *There seemed—and then no more of Thee*
>   *and Me.'*

'Nor will there be any more talk of thee and me if I have anything to do with it!' Serena said fiercely. 'Do they think I'm a fool that they should talk across me at table? I'll show them who's the fool.'

She read the fifty-sixth stanza.

> *'And this I know: whether the one true light*
> *Kindle to love, or wrath consume me quite,*
> *One glimpse of it within the tavern caught*
> *Better than in the temple lost outright.'*

Serena's breast rose and fell in an agitation which belied her name. She looked hunted and frightened as she paced the room. Darien had always been there since George died. He was the link with the old, happy past when everybody had adored her. She was now thirty-one and although she never lacked escorts—George had left her comfortably off and independence was often an inducement to a foot-loose male—she could not honestly say that they were queuing up to marry her. She had never allowed for Darien getting married to anybody else; his set bachelor ways were a standing joke to members of their social set. It was understood that when she decided to marry Darien he would be ready and waiting. Sometimes he had appeared to be on the verge of capitulation and she had enjoyed keeping him in a state of dalliance because she knew, in her heart of hearts, that being married to Darien would prove to be a different kettle of fish from being married to George. George had been a push-over, a few tears and he would agree to—or forgive—anything. Darien was implacable and would never bend where he had decided to stand upright and condemn. Darien didn't know her mean little ways, her habit of bearing grudges, her irritation with her son which changed into maudlin sentimentality and succeeded in making of her a Jekyll and Hyde personality in the child's eyes. He must never be allowed to know these things because he would then know the real Serena; and even Serena didn't care for her real self very much. Such people often live more happily in their public image than in their private—and true—one. They sometimes delude themselves by doubting that the real exists at all, preferring to believe, like some vain people, that the flattering photograph must necessarily be the truest likeness.

When she was calmer Serena finished dressing and then went in search of Dr Preston. She was carrying the Rubá'iyát and tossed it carelessly on Sally's bed.

'I think Darien wanted you to have this. He finds it

easier to borrow somebody else's work to play games with. I'm sure you do understand what a fool Darien is? If one laughs along with him it's always best, then he's happy and no harm is done. But I suppose you must be getting to know him, having worked with him for three months. I think you were awfully courageous, Dr Preston, going off with Darien the way you did, into the desert. Weren't you afraid of what people might think? Of course I know Darien, that nothing would happen, but not everybody does. He would absolutely hate anything to be misconstrued. The poor darling is really terribly innocent; the three wise monkeys rolled into one. Well, I had better go and relieve his boredom, I suppose. We always have such fun together. He did ask me to bring the Rubá'iyát along, but if I were you I would read a good whodunit while we're gone. Don't wait up. Jerry won't wake up after eleven. Thanks again for your help, and now I'll say goodnight, Dr Preston.'

Sally hadn't said one word. She couldn't trust herself. When the door closed on Serena Danely she picked up the Rubá'iyát and almost hurled it after her. Only the fact that it was an expensive edition saved it such a journey, and Sally, in her anger, had forgotten the numbers of the stanzas she was supposed to read without taking them seriously. She had lost interest in the project in any case.

CHAPTER THIRTEEN

SERENA managed very cleverly never to allow Darien and Sally the opportunity for a private conversation before the former left for Alexandria. She was not an early riser, preferring to stay in bed until noon, but when Sally, partaking of an early-morning swim, saw Darien coming to join her with the old expression of pleased anticipation on his handsome countenance, she had barely time to wish him good morning, with her heart doing peculiar things in her chest, when there was the shrill cry of a child yelling, 'Uncle Darien!' and young Jeremy was hopping about on the sun-warmed tiles near the pool, so obviously sure of his welcome.

'My mama told me she couldn't stick my chatter,' he shouted happily. 'Can you stick my chatter, Uncle Darien?'

'I'll have to, I suppose,' said Dr Marchmont, and began romping with the boy.

Sally told herself she mustn't mind. Whatever Darien Marchmont really thought about Jeremy's interruption he would never take it out on a child. The little boy was obviously spoilt. He would throw a tantrum for scarcely anything at all, but whenever Darien turned away from these displays he would quickly pull himself together and hurl himself after his hero.

'What made you change rooms?' Darien asked as they paused for refreshment after their bathe. 'Weren't you comfortable?'

Sally didn't know what to say to this. To tell of Serena's high-handed action might sound as though she was complaining.

'I think the boy is better facing the sea,' she said, 'and I can sleep anywhere, fortunately.'

'But you needn't have moved,' he derided. 'There must be five rooms all facing the sea. What a funny old thing you are!'

Sally said no more on that subject, she writhed silently thinking how Serena must think her an utter fool to have been so co-operative and so green.

'Cut along and change, young fellow,' Darien told Jeremy, who was steaming dry in the sun. He looked slightly at a loss as the boy produced a T-shirt and a pair of shorts from a beach bag.

'I've got my change here, Uncle,' he said. 'My mama said not to disturb her.'

'Then go and play with something.'

'With you,' Jeremy decided. 'I have to stay with you an' then Mama won't be worried.'

'Oh,' Darien looked at Sally with a smile. 'I seem to have a small, persistent burr on my back,' he said indulgently. 'I hope you don't mind?'

'Why should *I* mind?'

'Well, there is unfinished business between us, wouldn't you say?'

'Is there?' Sally had flushed and hated herself for it. 'When one has guests one must share oneself out. I quite understand that.'

'Frankly I'll be glad to get back to work again. Will you?'

'Yes. Can't I go with you to Alexandria?'

'Well, there's no need and you'll be company for Serena. It would look bad if we both pushed off, wouldn't it? I'll be coming back with our official itin-

167

erary and then she'll have to decide whether she wants to go back home or stay on at Inshallah for a bit longer. If we decide the boy could tackle a school then there's a lot to be done in a hurry.'

Sally didn't like that 'we' very much. She knew it was meant to include Darien and Serena.

'Wouldn't he benefit by going to school?' she asked.

'Yes. He must have some education in any case. Serena wants him to go to boarding school and be toughened up by the other boys, but I don't think he's quite up to that yet. I think he should attend a day school and sleep at home. As you've never attended a boys' boarding school I don't suppose you realise what little terrorists some of the inmates are. I was one myself. Anything as weak and whimpery as my godson would have received short shrift at my hands. Healthy boys simply don't understand physical weakness, and when it's genuine it goes hard with the weakly one. I can't allow Jerry to be thrown to the lions.'

'I like lions,' the child interrupted. 'Would you eat me for dinner?'

'You've got big ears, little pitcher,' Darien said, pretending to twist these members off his godson's head.

'Mrs Danely might insist on having her own way, of course,' Sally said somewhat acidly. 'The boy *is* her child.'

'I don't think she would flout me in this matter,' he said. 'She has respect for my judgment.'

'Of course the ideal would be for you two to marry,' Sally decided, and felt his gaze boring through her. 'I don't think you can be sure of influencing any woman otherwise. Of course I don't really know anything about it.'

'No, you don't. But I did think you knew I had other plans in that direction, or perhaps I misunderstood the situation. I can see myself and attendant burr are annoying you, Dr Preston, so we'll run away and play elsewhere.'

He stalked off towards the beach, pulling Jeremy along by the hand. Sally felt tears pricking behind her eyelids. She felt she had been small-minded and nasty and this man simply didn't understand or tolerate such things. She had resented young Jeremy's intrusion and allowed it to show, which was scarcely magnanimous on her part. She should have been patient and waited for all the magic to start up again. Not even Serena could take away what had been or do any real damage to two people determined on a certain enchanted course of action. Or so she fondly thought. She would be nice to Serena, gentle and understanding with young Jeremy. She wouldn't allow herself to become rattled or rise like a silly fish to the other woman's practised baiting.

But all this was difficult to remember when Darien was still watchful of her as the three of them sat down to luncheon on the shady terrace. Serena was looking lovely in a lemon silk pyjama suit which complemented her dark colouring to perfection. She was well rested and now ready to enjoy the rest of the day and half the night if needs be.

'As you'll be away early tomorrow, Darien, darling,' she suggested sweetly, 'I'm sure Dr Preston wouldn't mind us having another trip out together. It's short and sweet for me, whereas you two have plenty of time to get sick of one another, working together. What do you think?'

Remembering she had decided to be nice to Serena and keep her thoughts charitable, Sally answered without waiting for Darien.

'I shall be delighted to baby-sit again, Mrs Danely.

Jeremy was very good and only woke up once to ask for a drink of water. Do go out and enjoy yourselves.'

Darien was smiling or, rather, grimacing at both his guests.

'Then my evening has been decided for me,' he said. 'It's bad for a fellow not to be allowed a mind of his own.'

Serena took this as a joke and laughed, and the meal passed off pleasantly enough.

Darien had gone when Sally awoke next morning and she was conscious of the loneliness of this house without him; even thought how most places would now seem lonely when he was not present. She had to face the fact that if they were having a love affair it was a most unsatisfactory business to date. Serena had cut them apart as though with scissors, no matter whether that had been her intention or not. Sally had seen the road to ecstasy clearly signposted at one time, but at the moment it was lost to view again. It appeared certain that as long as Serena existed in Darien's life she could prove extremely demanding and damaging. It was as though she had her brand-mark on him and was not prepared to let him go as yet; with the ties of long association and her small son, she really had a very strong case.

When Serena deigned to rise she behaved like the mistress of the house even more than ever.

'Dr Preston,' she said over luncheon, 'I don't think we have much in common, do you?'

'Well——' Sally mumbled uncertainly.

'I know you don't like me as a person, and why should you? Women don't usually enthuse over other women. Darien suggested we would be company for each other for a few days, but no man can choose his woman friend's companions for her. I'm sure you would rather go about your own pursuits and so would

I. Is that all right with you?'

Put so very pointedly, Sally could not but agree and made her own plans with a certain amount of relief. She spent the afternoon at the hospital, feeling she had been away from medicine and medical matters long enough. She was shown some interesting cases, one being a case of leprosy on which plastic surgery was being used to graft a new nose and lips on to what had been a mere mask of a face.

When she returned to the villa she was told by the housekeeper that a young man was waiting to see her. She was extremely puzzled by this as she didn't know any young men locally and it couldn't possibly be Tom again, surely. The fellow was European and a stranger to her. He told her that he was a roving correspondent for the *International Clarion* and that a great deal of interest had been aroused by the story of the Melinda Lycett-Houth kidnapping and her (Dr Preston's) part in the rescue.

'When we reporters were told of the desert journey you were making when the news broke,' the man went on, 'there was also a great interest in the work of the World Health Organisation. Everybody has been waiting for you to turn up in some accessible spot, Dr Preston, before the story is allowed to die. You do know that Sir Wynford Lycett-Houth is most anxious to see you?'

'Actually I had forgotten that whole unhappy affair,' Sally told him, 'and I want no reward for myself. I heard the kidnappers had been caught and was very glad about that.'

'The active kidnappers were caught, Doctor, but a couple of their contact-men slipped the police net. It's known that one of them, an Algerian by birth, was smuggled out of Tangier. He is wanted for a number of crimes, robbery with violence and attempted assassination to name but two. I suspect that gentleman is lying very low at the moment.'

Sally said, 'Such things must be your bread and butter, but I like a quiet life.'

'You must be joking, Dr Preston. The last three months of your life read like pure fiction.'

'You know about me and my doings?' Sally asked in surprise.

The reporter smiled. 'We've been making ourselves unbearable at your Middle East headquarters, Dr Preston. That's how we have to get our news. We've had access to your log. The only thing the authorities refused to tell us was where you were spending your leave, but'—he smiled again—'they don't call me the "ferret of Fleet Street" for nothing. I've been commissioned by Sir Wynford, in return for the story rights and pictures, to produce you and introduce you to him. Would you be so kind as to accompany me?'

'Well'—Sally felt at a loss—'I really didn't want any fuss.'

'Then I would advise you to accompany me without more ado. Although I have a good head start my Fleet Street colleagues are hot on the scent and may turn up here *en masse* at any moment. Here are my credentials, by the way, in case you have any qualms about accompanying me; my Press card; passport—do you require any more proof that I am what I am?'

'No, of course not,' Sally said a little shortly. 'But this is not my house and I don't like to think of it being overrun by reporters.'

'Then take a bag and I'll book you into a hotel the minute we're through with Sir Wynford. Once I get my story printed there's not much point in the others hanging around. One's editor hates to print echoes.'

Sally explained the position to Miss McNeill, who promised to take care of any reporters who came to the villa. Serena and her son were missing, but the housekeeper said she would explain that Dr Preston was staying elsewhere for a few days but would let Dr Marchmont know her address as soon as possible.

'Where are we going?' Sally asked the reporter, whose name was Geddes. 'I presume Sir Wynford is in the vicinity?'

'His yacht is tied up in a quiet little bay about fifty miles beyond Benghazi. It's a good road and we'll be there in about an hour. I presumed to telephone that I would be bringing you. I hope you don't mind?'

'You're very sure of yourself, Mr Geddes.'

'In our job,' the man said as he opened the passenger-seat door of the E-type Jaguar parked outside the villa, 'one sometimes has to have the story set up before the event happens. There's always somebody waiting to beat you to it.'

The journey along the coastal road was uneventful and then, just before the sun dipped behind a headland, Sally saw a trim yacht riding at anchor in a half-moon shaped bay.

'Here we are,' announced Mr Geddes. 'We go out by boat. You've been a good little scout, Doctor, and I intend to give you a creditable write-up. I'll see that it's not too much of an ordeal for you. Keep close to me.'

The next few hours passed like a dream to Sally. There was Sir Wynford wringing her hand and writing a cheque for W.H.O. Benevolent Association, and all the while cameras were flashing and recording the scenes for posterity. Even the dinner aboard the yacht was recorded course by course, and Sally was relieved when gratitude had its say and she was allowed to escape into obscurity once again. Jim Geddes accompanied her to the Hotel Continental, a large white concrete building gazing blindly out across the sea a few miles west of Benghazi proper. The service was sleek and the accoutrements luxurious. It was all that Sally hated, but she did not hurl Mr Geddes' kindness in his face. Having an expense account he occasionally believed in making this expensive.

'I've booked you in as Miss Mary Smith,' he told her, and, as she looked at him blankly, 'The first place a reporter on the hunt looks is hotel registers,' he enlightened her. 'All exes are paid for three days. After that it'll be safe to go back to your friend's house. O.K.?'

Sally, who only wanted to sleep, agreed that the arrangements were O.K.

What international telephone lines were humming during the night she didn't know, but the very next day the *International Clarion* published the story of the aftermath of the Lycett-Houth kidnapping with pictures of the heroine of the case looking every stage from surprised to bewildered.

'That's just like my Sally,' Norman Preston told his wife proudly, 'to sail in and act, irrespective of life and limb. I'm glad they nailed that gang, I can tell you.'

Lucy said, 'She looks fit, doesn't she? I wonder when she'll be coming home? I want to tell another woman about the baby.'

'Another woman who will be its sister, remember.'

'Yes. There's a laugh. I wonder if Sal will see the joke?'

'I'm sure she will, and love the baby, too. She always wanted brothers and sisters.'

The news story washed over the shores of the Mediterranean countries and then made way for a political crisis in Greece. Sally felt relieved when she could put aside the horn-rimmed spectacles she had bought for a disguise and appear as herself again. She didn't particularly want to see Serena Danely, but she felt she must return to the villa Inshallah and find out about the work programme.

'And about time, too,' was Serena's greeting. 'Darien came back yesterday and was delighted to find two of his priceless tiles smashed, I don't think!'

'Whatever do you mean?' Sally asked.

'We had hordes of reporters here scrambling over walls and what have you. They damaged some tiles near the swimming pool and other things. Really, my dear, if you *have* to get your name in the papers you shouldn't be attached to somebody like Darien. He hates publicity. They were even trying to get out of him that there was some romance between you and him. He wasn't buying that one. The very idea!'

'May I see Dr Marchmont?' Sally asked coldly.

'He's collecting drug supplies or something. *He* works very hard.'

'The implication being that I don't?'

'My dear, if the cap fits you must wear it. You disappeared to enjoy yourself while he flogged himself. What *can* one think? There you were having the time of your life aboard a luxury yacht without a thought for anybody else.'

'Mrs Danely, I was aboard that yacht for exactly two hours, and they weren't very comfortable ones. I hoped if I wasn't here reporters would not trouble you, and I'm sorry about the tiles. I'd better wait and see Dr Marchmont.'

'I wouldn't if I were you. It's always difficult having words with somebody when a third party is present, and this third party has no intention of going out. You'd better give me your address and Darien can come and see you.'

'If you think that will be best I'll be at the Vienna Hotel. I'll take the rest of my things with me if I may.'

The proprietress of the Vienna Hotel was glad to see Sally again but sorry she hadn't a vacant room.

'Still, I will put you a bed up somevere, Doctor. In my sitting-room if necessary. Meantime you have a little walk, yes? Come back to dinner. Very special for this evening. I read about you in ze paper. You are quite famous, I think?'

'Infamous, more likely,' smiled Sally, now heartily sick of the Lycett-Houth business. 'Very well, Madame, I'll go for a walk.'

She enjoyed the first part of her stroll, glad to think that, despite any differences, Darien was preparing for their next trip together. Once they were clear of Serena things would improve in their relationship, she was sure. She tried not to think of Darien denying the story of a romance between them. She knew he would hate being questioned about anything so personal and even if their marriage was planned for the morrow would still not care to discuss it with strangers.

On the way back to the hotel she had an odd feeling that she was being followed. Whenever she looked round she saw dozens of brown faces, all the same, and all apparently intent upon their own business. Still, she found herself hurrying, glad to arrive in the familiar surroundings of the hotel without any ill befalling her. Ill was apparently awaiting her, however.

'Dr Marchmont was 'ere,' the proprietress said. ' 'E was angry not to see you. 'E say please telephone.'

Sally promptly telephoned the villa.

'What is all this elusive act of yours?' Darien's voice demanded like a sabre thrust. 'You walk out on Serena and Jeremy and then call and collect your things as though everybody has annoyed you. Has fame gone to your head, or something?'

Sally almost hung up there and then, but controlled herself.

'Miss McNeill must have told you why I left the villa,' she said clearly. 'It was not of my choosing.'

'Miss McNeill has had to fly home to a sick relative in Ireland,' he explained. 'I'm afraid she didn't have much else on her mind when I saw her. According to Serena you disappeared into thin air. We had to read the newspapers to find out what you were doing.'

'All that is most unfortunate,' Sally had to agree, 'but I can hardly explain my actions again over the telephone even if you were interested.' He didn't respond, so she asked, 'When do we go to work?'

'I wanted to discuss that with you, of course. Our planned return trip across Libya is wiped out. There's an emergency in the Congo and they're appealing for volunteers. That's where I'll be going. I'm flying from Cairo on Saturday evening with a consignment of necessary drugs. If your publicity stunt is over you will perhaps accompany me as far as Alexandria to be given your new briefing?'

Sally ignored the 'publicity stunt' bit and asked, 'Can't I volunteer for the Congo, too?'

'I don't happen to think it a good place for a woman as things stand,' he said a little more kindly, 'but the decision to go or stay must be yours.'

'Then I shall choose to go. Doctors and emergencies belong together.'

'The plane leaves the airport on Saturday at fourteen hundred hours, Alexandria, then Cairo. Perhaps you will have luncheon with me at the villa and we can then proceed together part of the way? Who knows, we may meet again at Brazzaville before we're sent goodness knows where.'

She felt happier for this conversation while realising that they had travelled a long way from the couple laughing and drenched in perfect harmony sailing a yacht together. She thought somewhat bitterly that Serena would wrong-foot her with Darien if humanly possible and that to all intents and purposes she had played into the other woman's mischievous hands.

After a lonely dinner she went early to bed. It was a long time before she went to sleep and then it was to have vivid nightmares which aroused her and left her trembling with fear. It was deep, dark night when she awoke a second time and this time a thin scream was stifled in her throat as she saw a flash of steel reflecting the light from the lamp outside in the hotel courtyard. A knife was hovering a few inches from her throat and the person holding it was hooded and menacing.

'You keep quiet, Doctor, or I make you so you never speak again.'

'What do you want?' Sally asked, her heart thudding like a hammer in her chest.

'I want you to come with me. I am not a man of violence unless I am driven to it.'

'But,' Sally temporised, wondering if this was yet another nightmare, 'I don't understand. You know I'm a doctor. Do you want me to come to someone who is ill? There's no need for all these terrorist tactics if that's the case.'

'Good!' the man said, removing the knife. 'That is what I call co-operation. Please dress and do as I say. If you give me your word of honour not to cry out or attempt to escape I will wait outside the window.'

'I give you my word of honour,' Sally agreed.

'Good! You English are quite ridiculous where your honour is concerned.'

He slid out through the window of Madame's sitting-room, where Sally had been sleeping on a divan, and she dressed in trembling silence and then joined the tall robed figure in the courtyard.

'Come with me.'

They travelled through devious back streets, stepping over sleeping figures and disturbing prowling cats and the largest rats Sally had ever seen.

'What's wrong with this person you want me to see?' Sally asked at length. 'Where is he?'

'All in good time.'

Sally pondered that it was most unusual for an educated person to behave as her companion was doing. When she paused to demand to know exactly what was afoot he gave her a sharp blow which sent her reeling and from which she never quite recovered until she found herself bundled down a steep, dark tunnel apparently into the bowels of the earth. In a fusty, damp little room there was suddenly light, and then Sally recognised her companion as he removed his robe and nursed the sickly flame of a paraffin lamp.

'You!' she gasped.

'In person,' he bowed mockingly.

It was the thug who had knocked her unconscious in the back streets of Tangier, who must be one of the unapprehended members of the kidnapping hang.

'I take it there is nobody needing my attention?' she asked, feeling suddenly clamer.

'Right, doctor. I wanted you for yourself alone.'

'And what are you going to do with me?'

'Nothing, I hope, for both our sakes. You're going to stay right here and be a good girl. You can even scream if you like. Nobody can hear you.'

Sally pondered the situation for a moment.

'If you want me to be good and stay here, what are you expecting to get out of it? I haven't even brought my handbag with me.'

'I took charge of that and a case of your clothes before I roused you. It really does look as though you left the hotel under your own steam. I even left a note which said you had been called away on important business. I agree that there was not much money in your bag. I am a man of expensive tastes. Perhaps there is someone who will be willing to pay for your release, however?'

CHAPTER FOURTEEN

As this sank in Sally suddenly exclaimed, 'Oh! So you're kidnapping me now. Is that it?'

'Mission accomplished,' the man told her mockingly. 'Consider yourself kidnapped, dear lady.'

'But I'm not an heiress, you know,' Sally said spiritedly. 'My father is a hard-working G.P., that's all.'

'I know all about you, don't worry. Getting your name in the papers tells all the wrong people what they want to know as well as the right ones. Since you were instrumental in doing me out of my cut in a very promising project I have had it in for you, Dr Preston. I'll settle for money—or your life. I'd much rather have the money.'

Sally felt as though she was in the presence of a cold-blooded, evil fish. Her blood chilled.

'How do you propose to get your money, then?' she asked.

'I'm sure you have influential and rich friends who would be willing to pay for your release. How about Dr Marchmont? All the information I have about him tells me he is pretty well lined.'

'Don't ask him for money,' Sally said quickly. 'Why should he pay you anything? We've worked together and that's all.'

'Still, it might be worth a try.' the other decided. 'Then there is the admirable Lycett-Houth. He is already grateful to you, and as you saved him paying for his daughter he owes it to you to get you out of this mess. I might make a bit out of you one way and an-other.'

'How will I know what's happening?' Sally asked desperately.

'You won't, unless somebody comes to release you. From now on I negotiate through a third party. If nobody pays then nobody will come and you will die very slowly.' He shrugged his broad shoulders. 'All is really with Allah.'

'You dare to mention God's name in all this?' Sally blazed. 'You're nothing but a fiend.'

He struck her sharply across the face.

'*Escut!*' he told her as she reeled back against the damp walls. 'Now do as I say or you will get more of such treatment. I am not an English gentleman, you will observe, and have nothing but contempt for English women. Take your pen out of your silly little bag and write as I instruct.' He thrust a sheet of paper before her on an upturned wooden box. ' "I"—whatever your name is—"am in good hands and perfect health. I hope you will co-operate and bring about my release. You must understand that if the police become involved I may never be heard of again and that will be your responsibility." Now sign it.'

Sally did so and her captor read it in silence.

'Good for you! I always thought a doctor's writing was illegible, but this is quite clear. You had better write the same thing out again in case I have to try more than one source.'

When it was done he tossed a paper bag at her.

'One full day's rations,' he told her, 'and I certainly hope you're not here any longer, because there's only half a bottle of rather dubious water in the corner there. I'll leave you the lamp, though it will burn outer after a few hours. Now it must be dawn, so I'll

182

go about our business. Let us both hope there will be happy conclusions for both of us.'

He let himself out and closed the door, bolting it on the outside. For the first few minutes Sally could only wonder if it was all true and if it could be possible that she might die here without ever seeing daylight again. It was too early for her to panic, but it was nevertheless a dreadful situation. She guessed that this hideaway had been built to house either a criminal or political prisoner at some time. It was probably built under the rubble of bomb-damaged buildings and might never be discovered in a hundred years.

She rummaged in her bag, from which the money had been removed, but there was nothing which seemed to be of any help in circumstances such as these were. There was a nail file and if the door had been locked she would have toyed with the idea of picking the lock. On the other hand the file might be useful in service as a screwdriver to remove the door hinges.

She worked frustratingly slowly and after about an hour managed to dislodge one screw. This encouraged her, however, and she set to work on the second. This was rusted and the small file kept slipping out of the groove. Then the screw did one full turn and the file snapped in half. At that very moment the lamp flickered and died. In total darkness Sally gave in to her feelings and screamed. She screamed again and again until she realised the futility of it, then she sank down on the wooden box and tried to compose her mind to prayer.

What Sally didn't allow for was that fate does sometimes seem to take a hand in our affairs. A sequence of events, known as coincidence, often occurs and shapes a different conclusion from that which seemed most obvious. So it was that Sally did not even know of the existence of one Ben Akerman who was to play such an important part in her early release. Ben Akerman was flotsam on the sea of fate. He was washed hither and thither, laying his head where he could and occasionally sharpening his wits when his body felt the need of nourishment. He boasted he had never, in fifty years of shirking, gone hungry. Allah always provided food for the taking. On this very day Ben Akerman had been watching the farmers bringing their livestock to market when a fine fat rooster had somehow found its way under his tattered *jelaba*. It had crowed its last, now, and he was happily plucking it and licking his lips in anticipation of the evening's feast. If a flat cake of bread should happen to fall into his hands then he would be replete indeed.

Ben Akerman had a small hovel on a bomb-site. A sack stretched between two partly demolished walls was his house and he was very happy to be able to live and eat without toiling as his father had done for so many years without seeming any the better for it.

As a thin, stringy dog sniffed towards the heap of offal he had drawn from the fowl he jabbered angrily. The dog had a wary eye, but was much hungrier than Ben Akerman and was now considering whether he could beat the man to the grab. All in a flash he had the rooster's head between drooling jaws, the beak hanging open in a voiceless protest, and was off over the rubble and away. Ben Akerman was likewise, howling horrible curses. It was only when it was too late that he realised the cur had not been alone. Its mate, in whelp, was now helping herself to the more delicate morsel of the discarded fowl, feathers and all, and as he bounded to save his dinner, made off in the opposite direction.

The starving bitch was ungainly and not very strong, but the instinct of self-preservation was still in her. After leading the man a merry chase she disappeared in a hole between two slabs of cement, even succeeding in dragging the fowl after her.

Ben Akerman was livid with anger. He would kill the bitch with rocks and then jump on her body. He would kill all dogs on sight in future. He tore at the cement blocks and went sprawling as one came away easily in his hands. He gazed into a tunnel of darkness which appeared to go down and down into the bowels of the earth. He was stunned for a moment at his discovery and then various explanations of the existence of the tunnel presented themselves to him, all pleasant ones. During the bombing, many years ago, somebody had collected together all the treasures of Benghazi and hidden them away down there, afterwards not living to tell the tale. There would be golden baubles and silver goblets and fine jewels. Or perhaps it was a food store and there would be sacks of sugar and coffee and tins of American food ad infinitum. Or maybe it was a smuggler's hideout; whisky and gin and brandy which one could sell to tourists and make a profit.

Ben Akerman was so lost in pleasant conjecture that his quarry, still with his fowl in her jaws, escaped and made off, this time he knew not where. He had to find out which particular brand of treasure trove he had stumbled upon. He would take a quick look now and then come back in the evening to remove it little by little.

So far all he could see for his pains was a steep, dank-smelling tunnel which proceeded for about thirty yards and ended in a heavy mildewed door with a bolt on the outside. Ben Akerman's heart beat wildly in excitement. He drew back the bolt and the door opened inwards of its own accord. At first he could see nothing as there was only a reflected light coming from the steep tunnel, then something white confronted him which the rascal felt sure must be a ghost. It spoke, but he did not understand it, and he did not stay to argue. He fled on rubber legs as fast as he could go, glad to see daylight again and intent only in putting as much distance between himself and the apparition he had aroused as possible. So it was that Sally found herself free and equally anxious to leave her prison. She didn't know how long she had been there, but the sun was now high overhead. She had no doubt but that someone had paid the ransom and that the peculiar ragged character had been sent to release her.

At the Villa Inshallah Darien Marchmont read the note from Sally with a peculiar sensation in the pit of his stomach. The messenger was the worst type of Arab, whom he had disliked on sight, shiftless, oily and creeping, like something which lived under a stone.

'Who did you say sent this?' he asked, to play for time.

'Oh, I know nothing about the matter, *effendi*,' another salaam, 'only that I am asked to deliver this letter and take the answer back to a certain house.'

'Which house?'

'I cannot say, *effendi*. I do not myself get paid if I divulge anything. I am only a messenger and do this and that for small reward.'

'What's up?' asked Serena, entering the room. 'You look as though somebody had died.'

He passed her Sally's letter.

'That's what's up, together with a ransom note demanding the equivalent of five thousand pounds. Quite cheap, really. She's worth a lot more.'

'But why should you be expected to pay a ransom? She's nothing to you, only your assistant. The cheek of it!'

'For your delectation and information, Serena, I am in love with the lady. I don't go so far as to say she returns my feelings. She's been blowing hot and cold, playing fast and loose with me. But I love her, and at a time like this it's brought home to me.'

'You're mad,' snapped Serena, looking pale and tense. 'After all we've been to one another you toss me aside like an old glove! I——'

He looked at her dumbly.

'What we have been to one another is scarcely relevant in this present crisis, surely, Serena. We can discuss that later. I'm only aware of ever having offered you my sincere friendship. Don't let's damage that relationship now. I'm worried sick wondering what to do.'

'It might be a hoax,' Serena said in a dry, cracked voice. 'She appears to like publicity. Have you phoned the Vienna?'

Darien left the room to do so, leaving Yussef watching the visitor. Serena went huffily off to her room and made a great show of beginning to pack. The proprietress of the Vienna hotel explained that Dr Preston had apparently been called away in the night. None of her staff knew anything about it. She had packed a bag, left a printed message and gone.

'Is anything wrong, Dr Marchmont?'

'No,' he said hastily, and asked himself, 'Where can I get hold of five thousand in a hurry? What's happening to her in their hands?'

At that moment he saw a peculiar vehicle draw up in front of the house and disgorge a weird-looking passenger. He could scarcely replace the telephone receiver as he realised it was Sally, dirty and without shoes but apparently unharmed. He was at the front door and scooped her up into his arms, allowing his heart to speak as he covered her face with kisses.

'Well!' she managed a watery smile. 'What a nice welcome. I suppose you paid the money over? I insist on paying it back, every penny, and—and thank you.'

'I paid no money,' he told her.

'Oh. Then I wonder who did?'

'I am at the moment being asked for the money. It looks as though you jumped the gun, my darling.' He looked her over. 'What happened to you exactly?'

'I was in the dark—underground. That was the worst part of it. Then a funny little man let me out and ran away. I don't say I wasn't terrified, but I'm all right. I sold my pigskin shoes to a man with a home-made taxi. I hadn't any money, you see.'

He kissed her again.

'If I'm tied up for an hour or two that's to let you know I love you and want to marry you. You can chew it over while I'm gone. I know you'll be hell to live with, but it will be all I want of heaven doing it. Now I want you to go quietly upstairs, have a bath and *stay put* in your room. I'm sending Yussef up to keep you company. Until I get the devils who did this to you behind bars I'll never be able to rest. Now I shall return to my negotiations for your release. From now on I shall enjoy it. By the way, if you hear Serena leaving, don't attempt to stop her, and that's an order.'

Sally went upstairs wondering if she was on her head or her heels. Had Darien really said he loved her and wanted to marry her? The day which had started so badly looked like turning into the most wonderful one of her young life.

She had a bath and donned a pair of Darien's pyjamas and a robe which a servant brought to her, then she sat in the room which had been hers when she was staying at the villa and exchanged occasional smiles with Yussef, who crouched on his haunches by the door. Occasionally he tugged the bell-rope and food and drink was brought to them. She wasn't bored because she spent her time thinking how she would tell Darien she loved him, too. There were so many variations of this theme that they were still occasionally occurring to her when he returned to the villa, and she threw herself into his arms without more ado.

Yussef disappeared immediately and Darien murmured, 'I hope it's "yes" after I've kissed you in pyjamas?'

'It is,' she told him. 'I'll try not to be hell to live with.'

'You can't help it,' he teased her. 'I'll never own a car without a dent, for one thing, and everything that happens to you will then also be happening to me. Life will no longer be tranquil, alas!'

Later he told her what had happened to the kidnappers.

He had refused, he said, to hand any money over to the messenger.

'I will only pay the person concerned,' he insisted, 'so you can go back and tell him. I must actually see Dr Preston before I pay a penny and then he can have the amount in full.'

The messenger, realising he was adamant, at last agreed to take him to his partner in crime providing the police were not informed. Darien said he would not contact the police until after the transaction was concluded and it was then up to the kidnappers to make themselves scarce. So he at last met Mahmoud Maxim, a very surprised and angry Mahmoud at having his hideout revealed. Surlily he agreed to take Darien to Sally. All this time Darien was carrying a parcel portaining to hold the necessary five thousand pounds. The second criminal, who had acted as go-between, was left behind at the house.

'I'm only dealing with one of you crooks at a time,' Darien insisted.

Mahmoud had taken him to the tunnel, found the door open and turned suddenly, saying, 'She's escaped. Give me the money. She's escaped, I tell you!'

'I told him to look around and make sure,' Darien said, 'and while he was busy I slammed the door on him and went to call the police. They're both in custody now, and awaiting deportation to Algeria where they're wanted on other counts. Now we can really think about us, sweetheart. Where shall we go for our honeymoon?'

'I really think it will have to be the Congo,' she told him, 'or had you forgotten that's where we're heading?'

'I had, but honeymoons are the making of places. I think the Congo sounds delightful. Don't you?'

She quite agreed, and to show it placed her lips against his in a long, lingering kiss.

Doctor Nurse Romances

Don't miss
October's
other story of love and romance amid the pressure
and emotion of medical life.

SURGEON'S CHALLENGE
by Helen Upshall

Sister Claire Tyndall's success as a nurse was
undoubted — but as a woman? Richard Lynch and
Dr Alan Jarvis both made it clear that they were
interested in her. Both were handsome and
determined, but both — unfortunately for Claire —
seemed to be married already!